Beautiful Evil
Winter

Kelly K. Lavender

Beautiful Evil Winter
Copyright@ 2013 Kelly K. Lavender

ISBN 978-0-9909431-1-2 PRINT
ISBN 978-0-9909431-0-5 EBOOK
LCCN 2013953136
Published and Distributed by Kelly K. Lavender Press
Printed in the United States

Cover design by Damon Za
Formatting by Polgarus Studio

For more information about Kelly K. Lavender, visit
www.kellyklavenderauthor.com.

Contents

Acknowledgements

Thanks to my successful husband, who always believes in me.

Thanks to my Dad and Mom for their love, commitment and encouragement throughout my life.

A special thanks to Mom for inspiring me with your love of books.

Thanks to Sara Kocek, a novelist ninja, for coaching me to play conductor to a symphony of storylines. The captivating result transcends my hopes and expectations.

Thanks to Polgarus Studio for the unwavering professionalism, extraordinary diligence and commitment to quality.

Thanks to Danielle Hartman Acee for her cogent insights and valuable guidance.

Thanks to Guy Kawasaki for writing <u>A.P.E.</u>, a must-read for any indie author.

Above all, thanks be to God for all the goodness in my life—my family, my friends, my horses and riding.

Chapter 1

"Will it happen this time? The ban announced last night—will it ruin everything? Dad says Russian law takes effect the moment it's ratified. I'm so worried, Ethan." I rub my eyes and lean my head back while the jet engines roar in the background. My head throbs and my hands sweat as we try to begin our 13-hour journey. We've been sitting on the tarmac for two hours due to a mechanical problem.

Ethan grabs my hand and squeezes it softly, leaning over to plant a kiss on my forehead. I gaze at his face, bags frame his red eyes. I look out the window to distract myself. It's a sunny cold day, the sky clear of clouds and full of promise for flight.

"One step at a time, Sophia. We're closer than we've ever been. Remember that," he says soothingly. Turning back to him, my body becomes rigid as anger spills over me like hot molten lava.

"You're thinking the same thing I am! We should be overjoyed at the prospect of meeting our son! This is a time for celebration, a time for effervescent bottles of uncorked champagne! But this do-it-yourself adoption is a nightmare! How much longer can we handle disappointment after disappointment? The closer we think we are—the farther away we are," I vent.

The conversation with Natasha on the phone last night burns in my brain.

"Adoption very risky in Russia now. The ban make Mafia watch money very close."

How could she say that on the eve of our trip?

I play back what Natasha said.

"This trip big gamble for you. I work to keep adoption away from Mafia. If I do not, police arrest you for human trafficking or Mafia take you. Better to go to prison. My name not appear anywhere, only yours. Phone will be disconnected. And I never know you."

"Hello, folks. This is your pilot I apologize for the delay. The maintenance crew is working diligently to insure the safety of our trip. Thanks again for your patience."

I glance over at Ethan, who's dozing now.

"Honey?" I place my hand on his arm, but he doesn't stir. Probably, the fatigue finally caught up with him, or... maybe he drank a cocktail, in which case he'll be comatose. I think I'll go to the restroom before the plane takes off. "Be back in a minute."

I carefully unclasp my seat belt and try to skitter by him without disturbing him. As I walk past the rows on either side, I glance at the tendrils of ear plugs reaching upward like small sun-seeking plants, and the hand-held devices, passengers attached to them like farmers admiring prized vegetables pulled from the fields.

As I reach the door, the occupied sign forces me to pause and begin to turn around. Suddenly, I hear the *click* of the door unlocking.

What luck! I'll just dash in and dash out. Hopefully, I won't have to hold my breath to stay in there. My face twists in repulsion at the thought. A haggard looking middle-aged man with a large paunch emerges and smiles too brightly at me.

That look—that look of recognition like I'm a favorite relative, but I'm not. His lids half close as he squeezes past me taking his slow sweet time. And he looks back at me before he stumbles down the aisle way.

Yuck.

I push the door open and inhale a shallow breath. The smell of pump soap greets me. All clear. I can breathe.

Ting, Ting. The strained voice of the stressed-out flight attendant echoes through the tiny bathroom cabin.

"Within the next twenty minutes, The Captain will be turning on the fasten seat belt sign. Until then, you can use your electronic devices. We apologize for the inconvenience"

Turning from the sink to the opposite side to grab paper towels, all 5'2" 115 pounds of me twists like a corkscrew to move around. A quick swipe of the towels, a glance at my nostrils, a push of the level, and I'm free to escape into the main cabin.

As I near my seat, I notice that "Mr. Too Brightly" is sitting next to Ethan.

Damn! I have to sit next to him! Looks like comatose Ethan has just re-positioned himself to face the aisle way. Why doesn't this plane offer two across seating instead of three?

My steps slow, but I don't want to wake Ethan up to swap seats since he's so tired.

As I stand next to our row of seats, Mr. Brightly realizes with a dazzling repugnant smile that I'll be seated next to him.

"Don't tell me you're with that guy," he says, gesturing at Ethan. "He's out cold." Between the screaming baby and me trying to wedge past him, he hasn't moved an inch." He smirks, his smile now a beacon of light.

I grit my teeth and carefully squeeze by Ethan's knees grabbing the headrest of the seat in front of me for support. Glancing back over my shoulder, I see him looking at Ethan.

I focus on the seat space next to him, zeroing-in on the instructions on the pocket pouch for my seat. Someone scribbled in red pen, *HELL A MILE HIGH.*

As I wiggle into my seat and grope for my seatbelt, he watches my every move.

"Lucky me!" he says as he cranes his neck over my arm rest to glance down my V-neck shirt.

"The flight attendant let me change seats. Person next to me was sick. She coughed all over me," he says, waving his hand in front of his face as if shooing flies.

A puff of whiskey more noxious than cigarette smoke wafts my way. My nose wrinkles in disgust.

"Now, honey, tell me all about you," he says patting my white knuckles which grip the arm rest.

"I'm too tired to talk." Turning away from him, I grab a blanket and reposition my entire body as close as possible to Ethan's seat.

"Okay, well, I'll get comfortable. Must finish my movie," he announces as he shifts around in his seat and loosens his tie.

From the corner of my semi-closed eye, I see him push off his shoes and remove his socks. Wiggling his now naked toes, he grabs his iPad and powers it on.

Gathering the blanket closer, I relax and try to drift away.

"Aw, Melissa, moan for me, " a breathless male pleas as he grunts.

"Yes, yes, that's it!" A female pants in reply.

A glance reveals more than I want to see, a totally naked couple pleasuring each other.

I feel my cheeks redden with anger. *There are children on this flight!*

As I glance across the aisle, I see a Mom hugging a toddler acutely aware. Her sour expression says it all as she positions her child's head in the direction of the seat window. Re-adjusting my body, I turn to face him, carefully choosing my words.

"Look, you may enjoy that movie, but a lot of people wouldn't—especially the parents of children on this plane. If you'll angle your screen toward the window and turn the volume down or use your ear plugs, I think several passengers will be grateful."

"Mind your own business, bitch! I'll watch whatever I want in the seat I paid for!" His eyes gleam. *He enjoys this too much.*

In my peripheral vision, I can see slack-jawed Mom across the aisle, her toddler now in the arms of his Dad. Her gripping hand like a talon, flexing as waves of rage engulf her. I see fury fill her eyes and heart—morphing her into a predator and a protector of her young.

Gripping the hand rest, I reach up for the call button. Immediately, his hand covers mine.

"You didn't say that you don't like porn," he says with a smile as his hand squeezes mine.

My eyes glitter with cold, hard hate—hate as tangible as a slab of black marble. Hate that maims and kills, without regret.

"Let me be clear," I hiss.

"Your movie disgusts me as much as you do! Leave me alone, and don't talk to me!"

Turning my upper body away from him, I grab a pillow and blanket—positioning myself toward Ethan and away from him.

"And I let my fingers do the walking walking walking—all the way up your back."

With unbridled fury, I turn and slap him with the force of my pent-up anger—anger at his moronic behavior, anger at having to

5

sit on the tarmac for two hours and anger at having to deal with idiocy all along this journey.

Chuckling, he touches his now red-striped cheek.

I glance over at Ethan for help, but he's still comatose, only a gunshot wound would wake him up.

Where's that flight attendant? I did manage to push the button. Some little kid is crying in the background. The 5-year-old girl adjacent to us is wearing white socks splattered with dirt. She's picking her nose and staring at us in wide-eyed wonder.

Finally, a tall, heavyset flight attendant hurries down the aisle looking irate.

"What's going on here?" he demands.

In a well-rehearsed move, he kicks Ethan's boot to wake him.

"What? Why did you kick me?" Ethan whines as he rubs his eyes, finally looking back and forth between me and Brightly.

"Good God, what's going on here?"

"I was just asking myself the same thing," says the flight attendant, shooting daggers at me.

Clearly, he thinks this is all my fault.

Rising to his feet and stepping into the aisle, Ethan blinks in disbelief, then grabs my arm and yanks me out of my seat to stand beside him.

"Are you ok?"

I nod, my lips trembling.

As Ethan turns to face Brightly, I watch him straighten his body and fold his arms across his chest, blocking Brightly into our three seat space. But instead of looking at the jerk in the eye, Ethan stares out the window behind his head.

Anger bubbles in the pit of my stomach, and this time not at Mr. Brightly. A thought that haunts me re-surfaces. Why is Ethan always so non-confrontational? You'd think he was Perseus managing Medusa. Sure, no one wants to brawl, but shouldn't a husband take a stand when it's necessary to protect his wife? I don't know what would happen if I was in serious trouble—trouble that he couldn't talk his way out of or rely on someone to fix. Got to hold on to the hope that his resolve would trump his reluctance— that he'd defend me. Looking away from Ethan, I grit my teeth in disapproval.

"What happened here, sir?" – asks the flight attendant as his eyes lock-in on Brightly.

"Well, I was watching my movie when this woman became irate with me." Leaning in my direction, he smiles adoringly, tilting his head to the right.

Slack-jawed Mom is on her feet now, pointing at Mr. Brightly. Her eyes full of fire and focused on felling her target.

"Who do you think you are?" she says."Shoving your garbage down our throats and exposing our innocent children to your trash!" Her moral outrage now silencing the once noisy cabin. Turning to the flight attendant, she continues—

"He pestered this woman. He put his hands on her!"

Taking a breath, she pauses satiated—even if momentarily. With a steady searing stare, she looks at me, ready to pounce again if needed.

"Thank you!" I say, relieved to have a witness.

"He was watching porn without ear plugs. I could hear it very clearly. When I asked him to lower the volume, he began harassing me. Then, he escalated the situation by putting his hands on me!" I answer, my indignation incinerating any thought of restraint.

"This man harassed my wife," Ethan says to the flight attendant.. He should be removed from this p-p-p...lane." He stammers." What are you g-g-g...oing to do about it

An opportunity for me, Ethan's body turned toward the flight attendant. In a flash, I lunge for Brightly. *Bitch deserves some justice.*

"Get away from me! Grab her!" Brightly shouts as he raises his fore arms to shield his face.

I feel hands on my shoulders now, pulling me away from my prey. Gritting my teeth, I resist leaning in, my hands a riverboat paddle wheel of slaps and punches.

"Stop, Sophia! It's under control now!" Ethan yells, re-doubling his efforts to tear me away from my quarry.

His arms cocoon me and pull me back—allowing the flight attendant to drag Brightly from his "foxhole" across the seats.

Ethan tightens his hold as Brightly stumbles into the aisle, grimacing. Brightly's face is ghoulish and green as his hand reaches out toward the seat back pocket to attempt to grab the small paper bag poking out. Abruptly, a cough and a stream of vomit flows from his mouth, clouding the cabin with the sour gut-twisting stench of onions and whiskey.

Catching the brunt of it, the splattered attendant gasps. "You moron! You're coming up front with me to sit near the Air Marshall!'

"Wait! I have something to say to him."

Ethan releases my arms sensing the passing of the raging storm that lives within me now.

There's no cup. Could use a sick bag, but that may arouse suspicion and possible restraint. Must be quick.

Grimacing, I reach toward the floor and grab a hand full of warm vomit from the putrid pool in the aisle. It feels squishy and chunky—my gag reflex glows bright red.

Swallowing hard, I hold my breath for a moment to fight the nausea. As I exhale, I pull his belt buckle toward my belly with my left hand while my right hand empties the vomit inside his fly.

"You want some action? Here's your action!" I sneer.

With a smile of satisfaction, I wipe my hand clean on his clothing.

Mr. Brightly is now red-faced and blustering, his pants dripping a brown noxious oatmeal substance.

"Let me at that bitch!" he shrieks as he swings his closed fist at me. Losing his balance, he lunges sideways and falls onto the flight attendant who grabs the back of his shirt and tows him to the front of the plane.

The child seated in front of us yells even louder now as the nasty fumes assault his nostrils. I turn on my heel, walking to the restroom to wash my hands several times and clear my head. When I return to my seat, I turn on the overhead air and glance at Ethan's disapproving face. His lips knot and his jaw clenches, signals that I expect to see.

"I know you think that wasn't necessary, but he deserved it. Get over it, Ethan."

He opens his mouth to answer, but then, shuts it, clenching his jaw.

"Yes, I'm aggressive," I go on. "I don't let people run over me. What will you do if you become a father? Teach your son to be doormat? Peace at any price, right?" I ask, shuddering at my words.

Before Ethan can answer, the pilot's voice comes over the loud speaker. "Good news! Ladies and Gentlemen, looks like we've been cleared for take-off. "

"Finally!"

Ethan settles back into his seat and closes his eyes again, as though he's off the hook. But he's not.

We're traveling to Russia, one of the most dangerous countries in the World and my perfect yet imperfect husband is as aggressive as a rabbit. And that scares me.

Sitting more upright, I elbow him. His eyes fly open again.

"What happened to you?" I ask angrily. "What made you sleep so soundly while all of that was happening?"

With a sheepish look, he explains- "At the terminal, when you left in search of frozen yogurt, I left in search of a pub. I thought I could finally relax a little. The drink just got the best of me. I'm sorry." Squeezing my hand, he looks out the window for a few minutes; then, turns back to me with an almost academic furrowing of his brows.

"As a guy, I can't blame him too much. He's very drunk and you're very pretty. I've struggled to keep my hands off of you at times. Besides, he didn't know we were together."

I raise my eyebrows in disbelief. "Are you making excuses for him?"

"Of course not," Ethan answers insincerely.

"What he did was wrong!" I continue, my cheeks heating up again with anger. "It was depraved and disgusting! Sometimes, you're too objective, Ethan. To the point of being inappropriate!"

"Remember logic and objectivity are two of the qualities you love about me." Ethan says with an endearing smile, fishing for a magic lure to restore the peace between us.

"You're digging a bigger hole for yourself!" I lash out, glaring at him. "Some things should remain unsaid. I hope one day you learn that. Inappropriate can create havoc for us in a third world country."

"But you know what I mean. You know I'm not malicious," he says gently.

"I do because I know you and give you the benefit of the doubt, which not everyone will do."

"I apologize. Please, baby, forgive me."

Looking deeply into my eyes, he grabs my hand and kisses each knuckle.

How can I say no to that? He's too charming.

"Maybe, one day, you'll uncap that big cylinder of swagger outside the bedroom. Having said all that, you know it's hard for me to stay mad at you," I mutter as worry imbeds in my gut, like a parasitic worm.

"I love you."

"I love you too, Ethan." I quickly peck him on the lips.

He chuckles as he entwines my fingers in his, his gaze now directed toward the window and mine toward the aisle. All is forgiven, for now.

As the pilot maneuvers the plane for take-off, Ethan begins to nod off, now snoring lightly. I, on the other hand, am wide-awake. Staring out the window, I can't help but think about all the emotional baggage we're towing to Russia, aggressive stubborn me and mild-mannered Ethan.

With a gentle kick, I wake Ethan.

"Sorry, honey, I'm so scared. Think of what's awaiting us—the people, the culture, the climate and 'no tell' Natasha as in 'no telling what she will or won't do for us.'"

Tears well up as I think of the possibilities. Clasping my hands together in my lap, I stare at the seat pouch in front of me as I struggle to stay composed.

"Come on, Sophia, what are the chances that something bad will happen? You've got to be more positive."

As I wipe my tears away, Ethan rewards me with a hug.

"Extreme uncertainty, extreme danger and extreme distance from home, I'm just talking facts not possibilities. Single out any one of the facts, and it's frightening for both of us, not just me.

Combine all of the facts, and chilling doesn't begin to describe it," I sniffle.

"Yes, both of us fear all of those situations, but we're beyond the point of turning back. The pilot won't stop the plane for us because we changed our mind about this trip. Commit to finding the happy moments and they'll be there for us," he cajoles, adding a chaste kiss to end the conversation.

"Now, how about a smile, Sophia?" He coaxes as he gently lifts my chin to plant another kiss on my lips.

Turning away, I cross my arms and stare out the window.

The jet engines whine as they push the plane across the runway. While the plane rises, my heart sinks.

Chapter 2

I lean on Ethan's shoulder and snuggle into him gazing out the window, lost in my thoughts—searching for a source of inspiration to bolster my sagging spirit.

High School … The only other time worse than this…occurred in high school. A turning point—the day, the event, the moment—that ultimately mandated this entire journey.

Everything changed in high school. Never thought my tenacity would be tested the way it was in high school. Never thought I'd lie bloody and severed in a pasture on the outskirts of town. Never imagined what happened could happen—neither could anyone else. When I think about my past, I remind myself—I'm just lucky to be alive and sitting on this plane. I could've easily died in that sun-scorched field in my blood-soaked clothes on the outskirts of Austin, at the tender young age of 18.

Looking up at Ethan, I smile lovingly. A deep sigh escapes my lips as I grab a blanket and snuggle into his shoulder. Absentmindedly, he brushes my bangs out of my eyes and plants a kiss on the top of my head.

"You need to sleep," he whispers. "You've already had a tough day. I know you've got this, but you know I'm right." He says as he kisses the top of my head again.

He's right. Sleep seems—as seductive as chocolate now. The magnetic force of it pulling me away from the airplane cabin. It's a match me and sleep—right here, right now.

***

"I'm sorry, you can't ride old Ben. He's lame. You'll have to ride King, the stallion. I'll ride the mare."

Hmmmm…I've never ridden a stallion. My instructor never talked about stallions, but I've only had two riding lessons—lucky to get those with 3 kids in the house. High school not the best time to be in love with horses. Needs prevail over wants.

My friends never talked about stallions, only geldings. I don't even know the difference between a stallion and a gelding. I guess it's okay, though. He's a horse, and I'm good with horses. And I trust Luke.

As Luke and I meander toward the 10-acre fenced pasture, King begins to toss his head and prance.

Well, he seems to know the way to the pasture. He wants to go there. He acts like he wants to gallop to it now.

Thinking nothing of it, we continue our journey, walking the horses side-by-side, flirting and laughing the whole time. As soon as Luke closes the gate, King lurches forward like a race horse at the starting gate. I shift a little in the saddle and quickly center myself, smiling at his exuberance. I didn't like that too much, but I can handle it and Luke can catch up to us.

Maybe, we'll get to race!

Instead, we canter happily in the open field. King becomes more animated, and shows more personality. Soon, we gallop across the field. King becomes more assertive and bucks, his head down in the dirt and his hind end high in the air like a rodeo bronc.

What's he doing? What the hell! Instantly, I lose the reins and cling to the left side of the horse in stunt rider position facing the rear of the horse. A jolt of adrenalin races through my body, like my first drink of hard liquor did. And the sudden splash of rubbing alcohol tingling on my skin sharpens my senses to a whole new level.

As King races to a barbed wire fence, I check my position by looking down. The ground appears a blur of brown, the horse's hooves streaks of black. My left calf hangs in the stirrup. My other foot and leg dangle freely. My bottom bobs toward the ground. My left hand grips the saddle horn as if it's a rescue rope on a cliff face. The hard, cracked earth beneath me amplifies the frenzied *clippity clop* of the horse's hooves. Luke's voice startles me out of my panic. "No! There's no time! Drop now!

But I can't. It's impossible to let go.

"He's headed to the barb wire fence!" Luke yells in horror.

What gives me a chance? Being shredded by a wall of barbed wire at a full gallop or dropping—which may kill me? No time to try to pull myself up and grab the reins. Even if I could, the stallion will buck again to launch me. Have to free myself from that one stirrup or I'll be dragged. Have to push away so I won't be trampled or kicked.

Dear Lord, please help me.

With a deep breath, I hoist myself up with the saddle horn. I kick out and push-off to lose the stirrup.

I want to live! I plead as I release my death grip on the saddle horn.

My butt hits the ground first at a full gallop, at more than 30 miles per hour.

"Are you o…kay?" Luke asks as he crouches beside me, his eyes glistening with fear.

I sit upright and glance at my blue jeans now deep burgundy red. I blink and glance again—I'm wearing the same dark red jeans. I stare in disbelief—there's no blue.

This isn't real. This isn't happening. I'm not menstruating.

This is too much blood.

"I'm not sure if I'm okay, Luke—take me home so I can check." Leaning back on my elbows, I can barely feel the crunchy grass beneath me. My vision is blurry around the edges, but I can see Luke's look of terror, etched on his face like a bad scar.

"You're going to be okay, Sophia," he says, "I'll be back as fast as I can."

Stumbling to his feet, he takes off running for the car.

It can't be too bad. I don't feel any pain. Maybe, I'll just go to the doctor and get a few stitches. It's getting dark.

Why is it getting so dark?

"Sophia, please open your eyes! I've got to get you home!" Luke pleads. Squatting down on his heels, Luke carefully scoops me up and hugs me.

"You'll be okay. We'll get through this together. I'm here for you, Sophia," he promises, his face twisted in worry. He hugs me again before cautiously, setting me down in the backseat of the car and speeding to my house. Mom isn't home so Luke uses my key to unlock the door. He walks with me, arm-in-arm, the short distance to the bathroom door.

"I've got this, Luke." I say bravely grabbing the door frame for support, but as I remove my jeans while positioned on the toilet, blood gushes from the area between my thighs. Slowly, I pull my jeans back on, my body still numb. This looks really bad, but I don't feel pain.

It kind of looks like... I'm bleeding from a cut artery.

"Luke!" I call, and he appears again instantly at the bathroom door." It's bad." I whisper, fighting back tears. "I've got to go to the hospital."

The hospital, Southwest Memorial Hospital, where my granddad died a year ago. Mom and Dad were outraged about his just-doing-it-for-the-paycheck nurses, and a doctor who proposed additional procedures on a dying man. I tremble at the thought of going there.

It scares me more than the injury.

Luke shakes his head in dismay, his face a picture of sorrow and despair as if he'd just run over the family dog. He moves closer to me. My legs begin to quiver. He pauses and gazes into my eyes for a few brief seconds, lost in his reverie. My thoughts turn to him.

He looks worried and disappointed—worried about me and disappointed in the outcome of the day, a day designed to be playful and fun. Instead, he's driving me to the emergency room because I'm bleeding like I've been shot between the legs with a 357 Magnum.

"I don't want to hurt you," he says as he carries me to the car." So, let me know if I do something wrong."

Clasping my hands behind his neck, I rest my head on his chest. I wonder if my blood is soaking into his shirt. I hope it isn't. He'll have to buy a new shirt.

I'm way beyond embarrassment at this point. Maybe, I can think this way because there's no pain—just lots of blood. I feel kind of drained right now, kind of limp.

Luke loads me into the car and rushes me to the nearest hospital emergency room.

"I'm going to tell your Mom that you're at the hospital because you broke your arm."

It's getting dark again. I'm drifting away.

Opening my eyes, I blink at the sound of a creaky car door. A concerned security guard hovers over me, trying to decide how to easily remove me from the car.

"Don't worry. I promise I won't hurt you. I'll get you out without hurting you."

Gently, he scoops me up like a mortally wounded child. As I lock my arms around his neck, my head droops on his chest. I cling to him as if he is a lifeguard saving me from a horrible death. My weak, bleeding body worries me less than the next steps through the hospital doors.

I hate hospitals. I don't want to be here. I want to go home. Granddad died here. I don't want anyone to examine me. I'll tell them what's happening. I don't want them to hurt me. I'm really scared. Where's my Mom?

My eyes fill with tears when he carries me straight to the emergency room. He lays me on the exam table with great care as if placing a newborn in a crib.

I close my eyes momentarily peer to take a breath to steady myself. When I open them, I see a middle-aged nurse with jet black hair, slicked back and pulled into a bun. Her beady cobra eyes peer at me over her clipboard. Irritation knots her already too thin lips.

"Lose the jeans and underwear or I'll take them off for you!" she snaps.

Oh, wonderful. I get the nurse with a coroner's bedside manner.

I grit my teeth, push off the table and waddle to the bathroom.

Stay tough. Stay strong, Sophia. You can do this.

In the bathroom, I stand and tug as the blood gurgles. My legs shake, and the blood pours. My entire body shudders like a building about to crash.

If this is a nightmare, I need to wake up now. I close my eyes and pinch my knees.

Wake up now!

The smell and taste of cigarettes fills my stomach.

Fight the nausea! This is real—survive!

I hold the handrail and wrap the hospital gown around myself while the blood streams down my inner thighs. I move in tiny steps toward the table. With a deep breath, I heave myself onto the table and lay down.

No more of that. There is no more strength left. I feel drained again. I feel limp.

"Spread your legs," the nurse barks.

"I can't, I just can't," I whimper.

Rolling her eyes, she glares at me.

Hot pepper sauce coats my tongue, and I feel the sting of rubbing alcohol again as my thoughts sink into a raging river of fear and adrenaline.

She's awful. I feel like a caged animal. I need to protect myself. I'll tell her what I saw. Maybe, she'll become a human being if I talk to her.

"I…"

In an instant, her cold beady eyes close. With a grimace, she grabs my knees—roughly jerking my trembling legs apart. A boulder of nausea pins me in place as I feel my body rip—my skin tear like paper.

For the first time that day, I scream and faint. I awake to see Dr. Weisberg, my gynecologist, at my side. It's shadowy dark in the room.

***

"No, No, No!" I shriek, awakening with a jolt to find Ethan cradling me in his arms. The other passengers are looking at me, the 5-year-old girl staring at me in astonishment as the fingers on her right hand dangle Barbie above the floor. Other passengers look at me as I gasp for air, tears streaming down my cheeks.

I was dreaming, and I'm shaking and melting down now—my head nodding in denial, my heart thundering to save me. The worst part of all is. It wasn't a dream.

Chapter 3

I grab a blanket and rest my head on Ethan's shoulder. He sinks into his seat, and I stretch my upper body cat-like to be closer to him.

So many obstacles, so much hassle. I'm so tired. Getting here, to this point, is a triumph in itself. I have to remember that...

Closing my eyes, another memory emerges crystal clear—that day last summer in the garage apartment office of my manager, Louise. Something very special about that day—epic, extraordinary, and landmark are words that only begin to capture its meaning. Ultimately, it was life-changing.

***

It's my lunch hour. Instead of eating, I pick at my cuticles. From the window of the garage office apartment, I stare at the street scene—trimmed trees and lawns perfectly landscaped by crews of men, nannies pushing strollers along the sidewalks in front of the large red brick houses with iron gates, gates which block entrance to part of the driveway and the entire backyard. Iron gates tattooed with a letter. Gates to keep people away from the sports cars and luxury SUVs parked in front of the garage. It's time to make the call. My hand trembles slightly as I pick up the phone. My heart feels as if it will bounce from my chest. I never call him while he's working. It's a first step, but it's a big one. I dial the international operator and give her the country code and number. I hear the phone ringing.

"May I speak to Mr. Warren please?" I say slowly to the Russian man answering the phone.

My father, a Vice President of a Fortune 500 company, spent most of his career traveling the world for his company. Dad designs and sells energy extraction equipment—the company earning hefty royalties for his top-notch engineering. He spends a lot of time on and around drilling sites, but dresses like a Presidential candidate when necessary to negotiate deals. Like many presidential candidates, he travels extensively—only on an international scale from Indonesia to Canada to Africa to Saudi. And he looks like a handsome leading man in a motion picture. Moreover, I'm not the only female who thinks so. Most of all, Dad is a wizard—blindingly brilliant—fixing problems with cars, plumbing and electrical, and enjoying the challenge. Growing up, a repair tech never called and never needed.

He was the natural selection to handle the revenue-rich Russian account; so, he began traveling there on a regular basis when I was a kid. Dad spent many a Christmas and Thanksgiving in Communist Russia without us. I hated the company for that. Year after year, we'd reluctantly and mechanically celebrate the holidays without Dad. It was like window dressing for a department store display. There were no Norman Rockwell Christmas Club moments at our home. We didn't own a membership.

But today, on the phone, I try to focus on the positive.

Later, that day he called.

"Hello" he answers, his response formal and brief.

"Hi, Dad!" I say, "Hey, I know you're busy, and this call is expensive; so I'll get to the point. Ethan and I want to adopt a baby from Russia. Maybe, you can help us find an orphanage? One that takes good care of the kids."

A deafening silence lasts for several international minutes.

"Why don't you just have one?" he replies eventually.

"Dad, I can't. Remember the horseback riding accident?" My voice falters.

"Oh! Yes, I remember... I'll call you later, Sophia. Let me think about this. Good-bye."

One week later, we talk again for a long time.

"Are you sure about this decision? What do you know about the subject?" he asks.

I know this tone—he's in attentive mode now. I can almost see his brow furrow as his mouth forms a hard line.

"Yes, we're sure we want to be parents, Dad. It seems like a natural direction for us. You've got strong ties to Russia. I've done some research, not a lot yet. I need to do more."

Finally, he says, "I'll look into it, and we'll talk again soon."

He's not on board yet, but he's considering it. He won't help unless he thinks about it from every angle.

While waiting for the next call, I begin doing research by collecting articles and information. I purchase a 20/20 video about Russian adoptions that is astonishing and scary. I watch children trapped in drab, stark environments with robotic care-givers, toddlers standing in their cribs, weaving back and forth, shifting weight from one foot to the other like a pendulum, a dance of emotional neglect which marks sensory deprivation moment by moment—no hugs, inadequate play, no friends and little toy time. Eventually, the youngest—the babies—lie still and quiet in their cribs, finally accepting the reality that their cries and need for comfort or love don't matter. I see sub-foster care situations, just a step above a scientific research lab. The punch-card clock and the bony budget win daily—a big glass of salt for the children to choke down every day, coating and withering the heart and soul. Later in life, these kids must often deal with a lifetime of learning and emotional disabilities.

"Have you considered surrogacy as an option?" my father asks in his-reserved-for business voice.

"Yes. Surrogacy in the US would be... risky and complex. A surrogate Mom with a change of heart can torpedo the best-laid plans and leave us with an empty nursery and the financial wreckage of living expenses, hospital and legal bills. "

Above all, how could I expect someone to do something I wouldn't do myself?

"How about a Russian surrogate?" he ventures.

A surrogate 13 hours away by plane doesn't seem reasonable, and a Russian surrogate living here could be tricky too.

"No, Dad, "I say, "We don't care about ginning our gene pools together."

"What about US adoption?" Dad suggests.

"Absolutely not. Have you seen the news stories about the adoptions that become nightmares?"

"I've seen news reports about babies torn from established loving homes at age six or ten because the birth father didn't sign the paperwork or the birth Mom wants her child back. There's no way am I signing up for that."

Dad doesn't sound convinced, "Aren't those the exception rather than the rule?"

"Yes, Dad, but we don't want to have that sword hanging over our heads. As a matter of fact, we have friends who adopted here. They spent $30,000 for the opportunity to adopt a baby through a private agency, and the birth parents want to see the baby on a regular basis."

"So?"

"Just think about it," I say, exasperated by the thought. "What if the birth parents don't share our values and religious beliefs? What if other relatives want to be involved in raising the baby? What if they disagree on our values and religion? It seems very complex and difficult to me to manage that situation."

Dad sighs. "I suppose you're right."

"Our friends also warned me that since I'm a divorced 36 year old, the agencies will frown on me as a candidate."

"Yes, I see your point. I know you must be doing a lot of research since we last talked. What do you now know about Russian adoptions?"

"A Russian adoption seems less complicated," I say relieved that Dad is finally coming around. "Especially in financially fragile Russia, few birth parents can actually bankroll a legal battle in the US; so, we could avoid a long, emotional tug-of-war even if they changed their mind and wanted to reverse their decision. Also, Russians worship cash—we have cash."

Dad says nothing for a few minutes.

"One last thing, Dad—finding the best orphanage is critical. A lot of these kids develop serious long-lasting emotional problems related to that environment."

"Understood."

"I'll talk to my Russian partners. And I'll let you know" he promises.

***

A squeeze of my hand and I'm upright, feeling startled until I see Ethan's face.

Where am I?

My eyes dart around to all the now familiar faces—the nose-picking girl scribbling in her coloring book, a baby sleeping in his mother's arms, and a balding executive reading a newspaper.

Rubbing my eyes, I look at Ethan.

"Are we almost there?"

Chapter 4

From Dallas to London, the first leg of our trip is uneventful. Next step, the London customs check. This should be a breeze.

Still sore and cramped from the flight, Ethan and I find ourselves with the other American travelers in a perfect square of a room, stark white from tile to walls to ceiling. The floor shows the only signs of heavy traffic, it needs to be swept. Several long fluorescent lights peer down at the passengers, and a couple of black metal frame chairs sit in a far corner, chairs designed for sitting briefly. The message is clear: get in and out before the metal starts beating your butt and your back.

Two guards stand like exclamation points at the center of the room beside a table long enough to harvest vital organs from living donors. They study everyone from shoes to ponytail. And then, they study them again from crown to shoes. Finally, they stare at your eyes and face like miners boring into a mountainside, searching for golden nuggets of guilt.

Ethan walks and stands front and center, like a proud soldier awaiting an assignment.

The guard grabs his carry-on, searching for "treasure".

The other guard stands about two feet away, head cocked and arms folded across his chest. He's a tall man with black greasy hair, long sideburns and a caterpillar of a moustache. He watches every twitch and every blink as if he would be tested on it later.

"Well, the bag is okay. What do you think?"

The guard motions him ahead.

I step-up next, pushing a stroller with a diaper bag in it. My stomach lurches as I realize that I look a little suspicious with an empty stroller. An uneasiness washes over me, like bungee jumping off a bridge for the first time. I feel my legs quiver.

Please no more delays in this journey. I can't be detained—not now.

"So, you're going to Russia," one guard murmurs as he circles around me, smiling.

"Where's the baby? In the suitcase?" He looks over his shoulder to wink at the other guard.

"We're going to Russia to adopt a baby," I explain. "I've got to be equipped for the trip home to the US." I stand tall, shoulders back and chest out, speaking with absolute confidence, a voice rooted in truth and indignation. My eyes lock on his and do not waiver.

"You know this is a well-travelled route for Russian adoptions."

I turn and glare at the other guard.

I have nothing to hide.

"Call Leslie so she can frisk her and give her carry-ons a once and twice-over," he says with a smirk as he turns away.

The guard in the corner stares, poised like a cougar ready for a meal.

After the London customs agents certify me as a clean bugger, I move out of the white room of inspection and interrogation. It's time to decompress after the customs "fun".

We begin to pass the next several layover hours in the cold terminal resting in black, rigid, hard plastic chairs. The chairs that some people nap or sleep on are as comfortable as a splinter in the thumb. Since we are too weary and too apprehensive to sleep, we sporadically pace and sit. Quickly, the polish of the American-based travelers begins to fade. Hunger pains, red eyes, wrinkled clothes and the disoriented mindset of international travelers replace it. Hour by hour, our carefully crafted appearance disintegrates as our situation strips us of our former identities in order to begin new our lives.

As the shine wears off the red ripe apple, the unseen rot of skepticism threatens to spoil our joy.

Chapter 5

From London to Moscow, the trip is easy and calm, restful like sitting on the front porch swing admiring the wildflowers. As we stroll through the Moscow airport hand-in-hand, we notice what isn't there. There are no t-shirt shops, no color, no bright or natural lighting and no inviting bars or restaurants. No enticing smells, just the smell of mildew and stagnant air. As we walk the dark, long, forgettable tunnel to customs, it seems as if we crossed a generational time line, not just an international one. This airport appears to be vintage World War II era, it packs all of the charisma and charm of a war bunker. Long lines leading to the customs agents add to our anxiety level.

Is this an old facility? Is this standard? A few neon signs and mouth-watering smells would be a plus.

The answers to my questions gradually become clear. Luckily, the agent waives us ahead after reviewing our passports.

Soon afterwards, Ethan recognizes our greeting party—Ivan, the driver, Viktoria, the translator and Natasha, the attorney. Natasha, a tall, plain-looking woman in her mid 30s greets me for the first time. Her short black hair and intense marble eyes compliment her full-length mink coat, matching mink hat and black leather boots.

The infamous Natasha—who told us multiple times she'd call us with updates and didn't, who told us to be ready to leave then told us to cancel our flight, who angrily asked for docs on a Monday and harassed us on Tuesday because she didn't have them yesterday.

***

How can we ever forget that agony?

"I call you next month because I think we ready then," Natasha declares.

Every night, we continue to sleep with the phone cradled between us, awaiting that life- changing call. Without a doubt, he already lives in our home. His toys appear everywhere, his phantom presence dominating our every thought and action. In every room, we spot reminders of our him—a crib with brightly colored sheets, a dresser filled with tiny clothes, Scooby Doo cups in the kitchen cabinets, rubber ducks in the bathroom, stuffed musical bears, trucks and Dr. Seuss books in the living room—all waiting for his curious little hands. To any visitor, our home appears to be a loving tribute to an invisible child.

I tear the calendar page and toss it in the trash; I carefully count every day and line through it.

Why didn't she call? I wonder.

Although we received distinct instructions in this bureaucratic battle-"Don't call me, I call you," I call Natasha anyway one day.

"We've bought our tickets for Russia," I tell her. "We leave in one week. We've been counting the days since our last conversation!" My giddiness bubbles over like foam on a too full glass of cola. Smiling from ear-to-ear, I stare at one very large packed suitcase standing beside the front door.

"Cancel plans not ready for you yet. I call you later," she replies sharply and hangs up. The sour taste of disappointment sits in my mouth like lumpy curdled milk for the rest of the night. Clinging to hope, I re-schedule our reservations for two weeks later and again called to confirm.

"Cancel! I call you in two weeks," she barks.

"Why aren't they ready? What could be taking so long? Did something go horribly wrong?" I ask.

The same questions at every turn in stereophonic sound.

It's Friday night about 8:00, and we just finished dinner. Ethan walks to the bar, an antique armoire conversion, within full view of the dining room.

"How about a vodka Collins?" He says as he mixes his drink. It becomes a ritual for us, as predictable as the sunset. Since we fulfilled all requirements nationally and internationally, we pour over the rules and regulations in an effort to determine a source of delay. Weekend evenings spent at a long rectangular dining room table covered in a white tablecloth of information and regulations, a heart-stopping heavy silence wedged between us. A raging waterfall of worry drenching us as the hours passed in quiet non-discovery. Sitting across the table from one another, our dull tired eyes meet. Holding hands briefly, we smile lamely at each other in encouragement. A stress headache starts to gnaw at my forehead. I put the papers down and rub my temples to buy some time as Ethan pushes away from the table, rubs his eyes, moving to stand behind me to massage my tight shoulders.

"Remember each day that passes puts us one day closer," he consoles insincerely.

"What's missing? What's the missing link?" I look over the files of documents and information late one night after Ethan falls asleep. While sitting in a white wingback chair with a cup of hot tea

perched on an end table, I pull a lamp closer to my teacup and tilt the shade toward me like a spotlight. One file after another is carefully stacked on the floor beside the chair. Each requirement checked twice, once previously in blue ink and once for that night in red. An empty teacup and a yawn mark the end of the first pass. I lean back in the chair, rub my eyes and stretch my arms out to my sides. The last folder on the floor is the first folder that I put together. It's titled "General Information".

Finally! Something to consider! The American and Russian requests are a non issue now. Everything was submitted. What could the Russians be doing or not doing? What does Russian law require? I need to do something different—look at this differently.

Line by line, I re-read this folder as a native Russian hoping to adopt instead of assuming the American role. The answer appears in a paragraph—the child must be registered on the Russian adoption rolls for a mandatory six months prior to adoption. When a family becomes interested in an adoptable baby, the agency must automatically place the baby's name on the Russian adoption rolls in order to allow relatives or other interested Russians an opportunity to adopt him. Russian law gives relatives and citizens preferential status during this period.

Suddenly, it clicks. There's no agency representing us. The child house does not have to put him on the rolls; so, they didn't. This has to be the reason! And Natasha never put him on the rolls! She doesn't know what she's doing! She's fumbling her way through the process, and not telling us about any of it.

Two more weeks creep by. Natasha doesn't call. One more day comes and goes. No call. "Too bad if she gets angry! We deserve to know something!" I say scornfully. I can feel the electric rage power on. My eyes narrow, fury pools in my chest. My muscles harden like rocks, ready to pummel something to dust.

Ethan's face tightens with fright while I grab the phone and begin dialing.

I'd like to rip your head off, Natasha! A lie by omission is still a lie! But I know I must get through this conversation without tearing her to pieces.

"Natasha, we haven't heard from you. Will we be waiting for 6 months for an adoption roll response?" I ask in an icy cold voice.

"No worry. He completely undesirable to anyone else. His medical records show many many problems, severe medical problems," she answers quickly, tonelessly.

"What do you mean? What medical problems?" I ask, terrified of her next words.

"He is healthy baby boy. On documents only, he show many severe medical problems so no one want him."

"What a relief! He's not afflicted with a long list of life-altering problems," I re-confirm. Looking across the room at Ethan, I see him smile warmly, basking in the glow of the day- brightening revelation. An irrepressible smile threatens to destroy my demeanor.

Okay, so, she basically admits to the mistake because she didn't dispute it at all. We're right. And yes, she knows that Russian disdain for physical imperfection would anchor our position on the list of prospective candidates. She plays that card just right.

"I call you in two weeks," she says to end the conversation.

Within the next two-week time frame, Ethan and I realize that Natasha lied to us in order to gain time, to avoid accepting responsibility and to cover bungled efforts. And of course, she doesn't call.

***

"Welcome to Russia. I hope this is the only trip you have to make," she says indifferently.

Terrific! I think. We are talking multiple trips now to make this happen, a long process and huge travel expense to go back and forth. We needed family help to cover these plane tickets. No mention of the legislative sword hanging over our heads. Is this about inexperience or ineptitude? Surely, she knows about the "closing adoption door".

I look at Ethan. His watery eyes mirror mine. I swallow with difficulty wanting to gag instead.

Returning home without our son. Dealing with another heart-wrenching waiting period. More false alarms and last minute cancellations. Nausea and intense anger well up in my throat like vomit trying to escape. I want to spit it at her.

As if to disrupt the loud silence, Viktoria, a fair-skinned, attractive woman in her late 20s introduces herself in perfectly British-accented, textbook English. As she flashes her best smile and extends a wool glove to greet me, I notice her simple, green wool coat, black boots and green wool hat. For some reason, she makes me feel more comfortable than Natasha. Her blonde hair and sparking green eyes remind me of a childhood friend.

Ivan grabs our luggage, and all of us converge on the waiting taxis. The 26 degree below zero temperature assaults me producing waves of shivers. I bet I couldn't be colder if I stepped dripping wet out of the shower into a walk-in freezer. I clutch my coat as I would a bath towel. I'm wearing 4 layers including silk long johns.

I might as well be naked in the North Pole.

The cold ices Ethan's mustache during the short walk from the airport terminal to the car, just our luck that this particular winter marks one of the coldest periods in Moscow's history.

With the heater working at maximum capacity, the windows inside the car remain frozen for the trip. I squint trying to sightsee through a sheet of ice while the van speeds down the road, blurring the world around us. In the back seat, Ethan closes the gap between us, putting his arm around my shoulders. He smiles a little smile with cautious hope in his eyes. And we venture further into the beautiful evil winter.

Chapter 6

The apartment overlooks an icy park bordered by a busy sidewalk and street. We climb two flights of stairs, no elevators in sight, to reach a landing with an almost airtight metal door, sealed shut with multiple locking devices like a bank vault. Natasha leads the way. Ethan and I follow, Viktoria trailing closely behind Ivan, who's carrying an extra suitcase. Like a human caravan, we soldier single file toward an important target. Ivan, a strong blockish, man is the driver and helps with any needed tasks. He's wearing a black fur cap and a very thick wool coat. We enter the outermost door to find another innermost security door with more locks. Looking to the left, I notice a small, simple, private bathroom with a freestanding bathtub and a gravity-driven flushing toilet. The tank rests over the toilet seat and a pull chain connects to the tank. Looking to the right, the small, crowded, dark living room area slaps us to attention with gold, brown, orange and white accents. A black rotary dial phone and TV set resplendent with rabbit ears adds to the ambiance. The kitchen, located directly across from the front door, intrigues me.

To satisfy my curiosity, I scan the area—no dishwasher, no coffee maker and no recognizable sources of nourishment. A breakfast nook area complete with a dinette set dominates the room, whispering intimacy and warmth. To complete the picture, a small, fall-inspired bedroom with tiny closets, completely utilized for storage, and a large double-draped window, all of which will serve as our home for a while.

Natasha huddles with Viktoria. They speak rapid fire Russian, the sound like high-powered machine guns blasting entire clips of ammo, a girls' club of two having a serious talk. "The rules are the same, Ethan. Do not answer the door. We will call before we come to the apartment. You always check to see that we are standing at the doorstep. Above all, do not leave the apartment without us for any reason. You stay here with the door locked until we come for you. You risk being robbed, kidnapped or killed or all three. Do you understand these instructions?" Viktoria translates and looks to us for agreement. Her demeanor and tone are both serious and patronizing, a warning to the mischievous children.

"Yes, we'll follow the rules," Ethan agrees with a sigh. "Will you give us a phone number to call you?"

"Ah, this is good. You not come here with my phone number. No, there is no reason for you to have it now. Food in the apartment for you. You have all that you need. You call me too much when you in the States," Natasha remarks with a roll of her eyes.

"Why you!" I growl as I step forward.

In a flash, Ethan grabs my arm firmly to hold me back.

"No, no! Let it go, Sophia. We'll be okay. Pick your battles— not everyone is worth the effort," he coolly instructs.

***

Once we "unpack", our luggage, clothing and personal items fence the perimeter of the bed, footholds are treacherous and difficult to find. Momentarily, I stop to breathe in the here and now.

We now live in another country, in another culture and in another decade, but Thank God it's only temporary.

Although our Russian friends consider this apartment to be very luxurious, it pales when compared to an American counterpart.

We're going to miss the comforts of home—fresh vegetables, M & Ms and Mexican food and the comfortable wing back chair in front of the fireplace. Not to mention the ability to walk out the front door to inhale fresh air and bask in the sunshine.

Nostalgia cooks and bubbles in the apartment as distinct and savory as the aroma of hot chicken noodle soup. Daily, we crave the luxury, abundance, effortlessness and comfort offered in our homeland—we even long for the celebrity buzz shows, news programming and commercials. In fact, there is no mention of the US in Russia news. Even more surprising is the type of entertainment programming available at almost all hours, vaudeville acts and soap operas. Stuck in the apartment for hours and days at a time, we quickly become TV literate.

Security is a daily concern. Moscow ranks as one of the most dangerous cities in the world, best described by the richest man in Russia "As the Wild Wild West with no sheriff." No doubt, strolling the city unescorted, without our entourage, would be completely reckless and dangerous for us.

Natasha and I sit at the kitchen table one afternoon with a few rare moments to talk about nothing in particular. We both sip our tea and gaze at the park across the street.

"It's tough for us to stay in this apartment for a long time. We'd love to see Red Square or the Kremlin. Can we arrange to do anything different?"

Natasha stares at the icy park across the street as if I had said nothing at all. The snow falls like confetti at a ticker tape parade. Sitting straighter in the chair, she drums her long red manicured fingernails on the table, acknowledging me in an irritated way. Her jaw flexes as her mouth forms a hard straight line. Her eyes devoid of warmth or caring, the eyes of a hired hand burdened with a very unwanted assignment.

"My job is keep you safe. No Kremlin, no Red Square and no Bolshoi Ballet. No sightseeing take place. Nothing."

Her gaze returns to the sidewalk.

"Someone died on that sidewalk yesterday. Murdered for the $100 US discovered in his pocket, a lamb eaten by the bears. Without us, you are three-legged prey. I have no time for play tour guide. I have more important job to do."

I swallow hard to clear the boiled egg of disappointment in my throat. My face and lips pucker as if I stepped on fresh road kill.

Okay, that was fun. No cheerful ambassador award for you.

"You know Mafia control everything here," Natasha continues. "Life, death and business at all levels. You can buy anything here—a driver's license, a university degree. Even a murder. You not on radar screen now. I keep it that way. Entertain yourselves in apartment."

I picture idle exhausting days. Our bodies slumped in the chairs, our eyes glazed over like TV drunks. The remote lying on the floor next to empty sardine tins, cracker sleeves and plastic bottles of that awful fizzy salty water, as tasty as premixed Alka Seltzer on tap.

So, we pass hours and days watching the pristine snow mask the dark side of the city, watching vaudeville acts in Russia on black and white TV, consuming mystery food and waiting to take the next step toward the realization of our dreams. In some ways, we feel so powerful to be in Russia in these circumstances. Yet in other ways—in all the ways that matter—we're powerless.

Chapter 7

Well, it's TV hangover, reading, Ethan didn't bring a book, or sex for the day again. Can't call friends or family and chat because of the expense. Cabin fever begins to get the best of us.

At 7 am, I stand looking out the window in the breakfast nook, dressed in my long pink square necked nightgown. My thoughts scatter like the unrelenting snow. I think about the man who died on the sidewalk in front of the park a few days ago as I touch the window and recoil in pain. The contrast couldn't be more dramatic—the toasty warm condo "jail" and the harsh cold park outside, where the snow falls in sheets like rain.

Ethan walks up behind me and put his arms around my waist.

"Good morning, Sophia. Are you ready for the day?" He nuzzles his face into my hair, inhaling deeply.

"Ready for another day of waiting? Blah…."

"Well, we can do more than wait" he laughs, squeezing me and pulling my hair away from my neck on my right side. He plants several gentle kisses there and then bites softly up and down the length of my neck leaving a strip of heat lamp warmth.

"Haven't we had enough sex? I just want to get out of this apartment," I whine.

"Just go with it. Or would you rather watch TV? Whatever you want. Last night was for me and this time is for you," he says as his voice becomes noticeably deeper.

I push his hands away and turn to face him. He cradles my face and kisses me gently and then more passionately, his hands moving like combs through my hair.

His hands drop to my shoulder. He pushes aside the strap of my gown as he begins kissing down my neck to my shoulder. He nibbles at my bicep. The top button holding my bodice pops as if by remote control. He reaches down and unbuttons another button.

I'm sunk now.

Looking down, smiling like a miner with newly discovered treasure, Ethan's eyes soften. I bite my lower lip and look up at him looking at me. My breathing becomes louder and more erratic while his becomes slower and more deliberate.

My gown falls a little closer to the floor and my barely contained cleavage strains to be released. He drops his other hand and strokes the front of my neck, stopping at the hollow. The oven warmth travels. A slow explorative kiss at the hollow. Slowly, he draws an "S' shape on my chest close to my cleavage. A kiss above the opposite collarbone and one more push of fabric toward my elbow. Just breathing would make it fall. The oven becomes a hot tub of bubbly heat. Ethan scoops me into his arms and carries me into the bedroom.

***

At 9 am, Natasha calls to tell us she'll be stopping by.

"We travel today," she announces when she arrives at the front doorstep wearing a fur coat, a matching fur hat and black leather gloves.

"You must make ready to go outdoors."

Ethan and I look at each other, excited and relieved.

Natasha walks to the hall closet, grabs a full-length mink coat, and hands it to me along with a silk Chanel scarf.

"Wear this and wrap the scarf around your head and neck like mine."

As happy as I am about the prospect of leaving the apartment, I bristle at the hypocrisy of me wearing fur.

My family would howl with laugher now, the vegan wearing fur.

Natasha's supercilious stare feels like sunburn.

"Is there a problem?" she asks, her voice laced with anger.

Another culture. It's too difficult to explain my choice. It may be insulting to her to refuse to wear the coat. Have to abandon my vegan nature here in this frozen tundra or shiver and starve. Be gracious. The best policy as Mom would say.

"Oh no, it's beautiful, I've just never had the chance to wear such an expensive coat." As I slip it on, I can almost hear the giggles and laughter.

"You be glad you wear this today." Natasha comments with a half smile. We descend the stairs to street level. Natasha examines her vehicle, a Hyundai, buried beneath inches of snow. "Go back upstairs and wait while I clear snow, "she instructs. Within twenty minutes, she returns to the apartment to escort us back to the car.

"And this is my car. "She extends her hand toward the vehicle as if introducing the latest in Lamborghini at a car show. Before opening the car door, she de-activates the car alarm.

"I had a special expensive alarm installed," she says smugly.

She seems so awe-stuck by that car. I mean a Hyundai is not a Bugatti.

Her lips and face tighten as she registers the apparent surprise on my face.

"Here in Russia cars very expensive and very valuable. We can't borrow money to buy a car or home. We must to save the money for large purchases."

Turning away from me as if to dismiss my ignorant response, she presses down hard on the accelerator. The car tires claw out of the street side space. A plume of snow marks our escape. And the car roars down the milky white street.

As we travel the icy roads seat beltless, seatbelts not an option, we discuss the next stop—the child house.

Chapter 8

It's two in the afternoon after a long drive to the airport, and we're boarding a plane to go somewhere. The trek to the child house is surreal. It seems like a hallucination anchored by a shot of tequila and a pickled worm. As we board the plane, a large dog sitting in a first class seat catches my eye. The dog sits happily positioned next to his owner, and no one gawks except us.

After we settle into our seats, the first pint of liquor appears. Someone sitting behind me shoves a bottle into my seat space.

That's really odd—passengers carrying liquor and drinking it on the plane. I look at Ethan with my "what do I do now?" eyes. His head rolls back and he laughs at the absurdity of it all.

"He's offering you a drink," he says smiling.

"Yes, I am offering both of you a drink," the man says in textbook perfect English.

"Where are you from?" I ask curling my body around from my aisle seat.

"We're from New Zealand" the white-haired clean-shaven man replies. He doesn't look a day over 50. Smiling, he offers us the bottle again. His wife has both arms curled around him in an affectionate hug. She smiles and looks intently at us, gauging our response to the offer.

I pass the bottle to Ethan who accepts the offer and passes it back to me. *Ewww…! Seeing him drink from that pint is almost as surprising as seeing the pint being shared in the first place.*

"I'll pass, thanks," I say handing it back with my lips tightly pressed together.

"Look, he's passing it down to the next row of seats across from us," I lean over and whisper to Ethan.

"How could you drink after a bunch of strangers?"

He shrugs. "Liquor is alcohol-based. There's no germ issue. It's strong enough to kill anything in its path. Your mouth will be cleaner after you drink actually."

"Hmmm…never thought of it that way," I say.

"Ewww…!"

"What? "

"Water is dripping on my head!" I say. "And it feels like a worm of sticky slime is inching down the middle of my back." I run my hand across my hair and grimace.

"The ceiling is apparently dripping water," says Ethan. "Probably condensation."

As I glance around the plane, several passengers enjoy their favorite "poison" on board and drink liberally. The plane drips in several places and makes creaky, groaning noises—complaining like a VW bug trying to pull a flat bed filled with iron pipe up a mountainside.

"Wonderful! I mutter "Chinese water torture with no escape."

I drink from the pint this time, stand up and hand it to Ethan.

No wonder everyone drinks on these flights! We have to rely on a worn-out squeaky leaky airplane to haul us up through the clouds.

A few passengers coax us into sampling their favorite liquors. It's a pass the bottle, gulp and smile party game with the passengers across the aisle. The liquor sedates and calms us as we cope with the unsettling drips that fall from the plane ceiling and the sounds of struggle as the hard-working aircraft makes a Herculean effort to reach its destination. In just an hour, we begin to disembark.

Rickety as the Russian plane is, I can't help but admit to myself as we climb down the steps that the flight was more fun than the US first-class, hot towel, warm nuts and freshly baked chocolate chip cookie, experience going to Russia.

Ethan and I walk slow alcohol-pickled steps on the ice-covered metal stairs and concrete runway while other passengers rush around us. We move like senior citizens caught in the path of Boston Marathoners. Natasha quickly hails two taxis, one for people and one for luggage, and we race along the glacial roads to our hotel.

Even though we stay in the best hotel in the city, the hallways and common areas are not heated. Extra rolls of toilet paper, with the texture of commercial grade paper towels, are provided sparingly and only when requested. Since cleaning staff only cleans rooms by daily request, Ethan and I scout regularly for cleaning assistance and cleaning supply rooms, to build toilet paper reserves. Also, of course, if illness strikes, leech therapy, blood suckers attached to remove any toxins, are always available in the lobby for the asking. And if questions arise about safety or security, a group of uniformed policemen huddle in the lobby on a daily basis.

"Natasha, is there an exercise room?" I ask eagerly.

"This is best hotel in area! No, there is no exercise room!" Natasha answers, her brow furrowing. Obviously, I've insulted her once again.

"Can I run the stairs for exercise?" I persist, looking at her squarely in the eyes.

"No, you cannot. The cold can permanently damage your lungs if you do that, no heat in the stairwells." She smiles a tiny smile, but her eyes are straight lines. And with that, she buttons her coat and tightens her scarf, throwing the long end over her shoulder like a feather boa. Then, she spins on her heel to leave, dismissing us from her radar for the time being.

The invalid stay-in-your-room program in Moscow drives me stir crazy. Only a broken back would be more limiting.

For fun, we treat ourselves to the heated pool experience; however, at an ice cold 40 degrees, it proves too numbing. As I bolt from the pool, I feel the immediate smoky cold embrace of the unheated indoor common area surrounding the perimeter of the pool. I scramble to remove the wet bathing suit while I hide behind a freestanding bar.

If I could swim in wintry Lake Michigan naked, I might stand a chance in this country. My body can handle hot tropical weather, but I become a human Popsicle here.

Ethan, who enjoys wearing short-sleeved shirts year-round, races away from the area minutes before I do. In the room, our bodies thaw completely as we entangle ourselves in an oasis of pillows, blankets and sheets.

Thinking back to years before, we lived our daily lives together yet apart. Although we shared the same roof, we orbited around one another. He pursued his weekend activities with his friends, hunting and fishing and I pursued my weekend activities, riding lessons, horse shows and reading. Aside from our common goals to pay-off the mortgage early and maintain our property, we share very little, especially quality spare time. We loved one another, but we became lazy about our relationship. Only the work toward the adoption forced us to share our feelings and our lives more with one another.

Now, our stressful, isolated situation in Russia presents the perfect opportunity to re-discover one another. To my pleasant surprise, our relationship begins to grow in some long forgotten ways.

Chapter 9

Lying in bed, side-by-side cuddling, I reminisce about the first time I met Ethan. Snuggling into him, I feel the flutter of butterflies, and it all comes back to me.

***

Barbara, a petite smart blonde, tilts her head and listens with empathy and concern as I tell her about my Senior Level Finance course jitters. We sit outside on a bench in front of the business school. Some students lounge underneath trees around us, reading books or observing the passer-bys. Others play Frisbee in a large grassy clearing in front of a splashing fountain and wading pool. It's a perfect day to be a young college student. Life leaps at you from every direction and the warm sunlight spotlights every moment. It doesn't matter to me. This one class just worries me a lot, it's rumored to be as tough and dry as a leather bull whip.

"I know someone who just finished that class. He may have some old tests," Barbara offers. "I'll ask him and let you know."

One week later, Barbara and I cross paths in the library-the quiet, busy beehive for serious students. Turning to me, she says, "Sophia, I'd like for you to meet Ethan. Ethan just finished that course we talked about."

I automatically lower my eyes and wince at the thought of having to deal with another "great guy;" then, starting with his shoes, I slowly gaze at this person who stands before me. Six foot tall with dark brown hair, forest green eyes and a hairy chest peeking at me through his shirt. He had a good body and a confident, relaxed demeanor.

Hmmm…

A familiar sensation of warm steamy towels strategically placed in thong bikini formation across my breasts and my midriff sets in, and lust beckons with a big smile. Then, an invisible restraint triggers, the think-with-your-brains-not-your-biology safety switch. The fortress gates close in a flash, and a battalion of hormones standing ready to engage, turn abruptly and walk away.

Barbara elbows me back to reality as Ethan waits for me to introduce myself. I look directly into his eyes. He puts me at ease.

Maybe, he is okay unlike cheating Eric, the last guy I felt drawn to. Men are a flaming hot topic for me now.

"Hello, my name is Sophia," I say with a firm handshake.

"I'm just beginning the course you finished, and I think forming a Finance Major Alliance might benefit both of us. Will you give me your number so we can discuss classes?"

With an impish smile and a nod, he scribbles his number on a piece of paper, adding in a serious tone, "Don't give this number out to a bunch of girls. I don't want a lot of girls calling me."

How's that for conceit and arrogance? Ring the bell—another jerk.

A few weeks pass, then, one day, he walks down the empty hallway as I stand outside my next class. The faded pastel blue walls and closed wooden doors seem to showcase his arrival—like a stage setting in a play.

I cover my mouth and look at the floor to hide a smile.

It never fails, now I'll see him everywhere.

"Hi! Hey, you need to give me your phone number so we can get together," he says in a very happy, disarming way. A few seconds pass as I try to understand his surprising pleasantness. After all, I haven't called him in weeks.

Is he that easy-going?

Maybe, he's worth talking to after all; so, I give him my parent's phone number to keep him at a distance.

During the next three weeks, he calls me and calls me, but I'm never home, of course. I live apart from Mom and Dad. Mom and Dad live on the 25th floor in a luxury condo downtown. It's beautifully decorated in warm earth tones and velvety soft furniture. A beautiful chandelier hangs over the walnut dining room table. One floor above is the penthouse suite, used to film a scene in *The Urban Cowboy* movie. A sense of wonder and giddiness envelopes me every time I step out on the balcony. One day a few years ago, when Mom, Dad and I sat on the cushy furniture visiting, a helicopter hovered close to the balcony railing like a spy trying to hear a snippet of the conversation.

Well, anyway, Mom always gives me the message that Ethan called. And I always toss it. For some reason, I just don't want to talk to him.

Finally, one day, when visiting with my Mom, she says, "What's going on with this guy, Ethan? He leaves a lot of messages here. Do you ever call him back?"

"No, Mom," I sigh."I don't know what to think of him. He seems okay, but men make me sprint in the opposite direction now."

I tell her about our first meeting. Mom knows I feel "fried "after Eric.

"He's a nice guy, Sophia. I talked to him several times. I'm tired of taking these messages. You call him now!" my mother barks, thrusting the latest message in my face. I grab the message with a tight grimace and skulk all the way to the next room like some child told to eat her entire portion of broccoli casserole. When I enter my room, a broad smile replaces the petulance. I push my door as far as possible against the backstop. Now, my bedroom door is wide open.

When Ethan answers his phone, I speak extra loud so Mom can hear me all the way downstairs.

"Well, Ethan, I'm calling you because my mother is tired of taking messages. Now, if she and my Dad leave the house, we can have wild animal sex on the rug in front the fireplace or maybe we can use their bed. By the way, how many kids do you want to have? How much money does your Dad earn? What does your mother do? When do you want to be engaged?" *It's important that Mom hear every word.*

"*Well,* why don't you spend some time with me to find out the answers to your questions?" He answers with a chuckle.

"This might be a fun date." I think after he spells out a time and day. I lean into the phone. "Where would we be going?" I ask as my mind races, a nice restaurant or a movie and an ice cream parlor?

"Let's go to a pizza place," Ethan says in a matter of fact way. "Amy is going with us."

"I don't …understand. I thought we were going out on a date," I stammer.

"Noooo…We are just all getting together in a study group with old tests," Ethan explains.

"Well, that changes my goals. No sex in front of the fireplace and no engagement," I comment, aglow in crimson red.

"You know I really need to go. Good-bye, Ethan."

What a relief! I really don't know what to think of this guy!

"Wait, I do want to take you out on a date, just me and you. How about it?"

"I don't think so."

"Come on and say yes. We'll have fun. I do want to spend some time with you," he coaxes. Once again, I listen for and hear the honesty in his voice.

"You seem like a nice guy," I say at last. "but I'm feeling very wicked right now after my last relationship. "The answer is 'no' today and 'no' six months from today. Go away, Ethan."

***

I'm beaming. It's so different now. With a giggle, I grab my pillow and begin to pummel him. Changing the temperature in the chilly hotel room is all fun and games, tropical, balmy and steamy. We're doing our part to warm-up our space in Siberia.

No harm, no foul. Right?

Chapter 10

Ethan slips out of bed—grabbing his clothes from the floor. Slithering across the rumpled mattress, I slap his bare bottom. Glancing over his shoulder, he gives me a dirty smirk. Gathering the covers around my head, I giggle and remember....

***

It just so happens our first date falls on Valentine's Day. We go to dinner and a movie. We talk, laugh and tease each other the whole time.

"Well, I guess you'll have to eat beans for the rest of the month to pay for this date," I joke as he pays for the movie tickets.

"No, I only have to go without electricity and water next month. I can always raid my parent's home for food," he banters back.

After the movie, he asks me to stop by his house to meet his roommates. As I walk in the front door, he trails behind me. Then, he sweetly says, "Happy Valentine's Day!" and as I turn to face him, he presents me with a rose. I smile and feel a little tingle run up and down my spine.

Who is this guy? He's so unlike any guy I ever dated or met. He's kind and charming.

More lengthy phone calls and dates fill the rest of the semester and the next semester. And before I know it, I have the answer to that question. When I'm with him, I feel the embrace of a warm bath. I relax and smile and drift through the day, a sense of timelessness carrying me along. I felt warm, clean, soft and naked in my clothes. The huge fortress guarding my heart begins to gradually open its gates, the sharpshooters standing at ease by their weapons. As time passes, the marksmen sleep by their weapons or leave their posts unattended, the gates always stay open. There is need to defend against Prince Charming.

***

Yes, Ethan is special-attractive, funny, sweet, smart and caring.

I fell in love.

And it's as magical now as it was then.

Stretching my arms and covering my yawn, I smile sweetly and roll—over to grab my clothes. In our hotel room, entertainment becomes a daily question mark. The cold nights are especially fun, but the days drag along. Looking out from the balcony, the tall pine-like trees dressed in long snowy white coats stand everywhere watching us, swaying like dancers in a choreographed Broadway show. The cold white snow covering the ground is as seductive as vanilla ice cream. It beckons to us to play outside for snowball warfare or a two-person roll and kiss. A snow angel will be fun to make when the wind stops. A mouthful of snow would be delicious or the chance to surprise Ethan with a handful in his hair.

Snow even laces the windows facing the outdoors. It has to be a bit warmer for snow games. I prefer indoor games when the weather is this cold. My body craves something physical, but

Natasha insists no exercise because I risk permanently damaging my lungs.

Lying next to Ethan at the footboard, my elbows sink into the mattress like anchors as my knitted fingers support my frowning face.

Being bored and waiting – it stinks!

Looking at Ethan look at me, I know that the wheels are turning in his brain.

"I've got it!" I say, throwing caution to the wind. "Let's play hustle games in the bar downstairs."

"I'll pick you up first," he adds darkly.

***

"One more thing—lipstick." I lean into the mirror and apply the pink pastel color—no smeared eyeliner, no sand-size fragments of black mascara peppering the skin under my lower lashes. Brown eyes clear, bright, and brown hair smooth, straight and shiny.

Another quick check—jeans zipped, pink Angora turtleneck collar okay, gold chandelier faux diamond earrings and black cowboy boots. A quick check of the soles and heels indicate I wouldn't be walking in with toilet paper stuck to my shoe.

Ethan will leave the room about 15 minutes after me.

The smoky, dimly lit bar—a scaled down version of a Texas Honky Tonk with Mafioso, Viktoria whispered to me, instead of cowboys. The cloud of cigarette smoke clings to the ceiling while the sounds of dance music and raucous laughter fill the room. A dirty white linoleum floor streaked by black scuffmarks reminds me more of a busy restaurant kitchen floor than that of a bar. A big gilded mirror covers most of the wall facing the wooden bar. Bottles of liquor sit on the counter underneath the mirror. The black leather bar stools line up in front of the bar, and a handful of small wooden tables dot the small space.

I hope no one tries to talk to me. I don't speak enough Russian to carry on a conversation or to respond to a drunk.

My steps quicken at the thought.

Let's get this over with!

With my chest out and shoulders back, I push through the barrier of quarter-length swinging doors and walk confidently into the bar.

> "Hell is empty and all the devils are here."
> —William Shakespeare

Chapter 11

Not many women here just, a 60ish bleached blonde with a Louis Vuitton handbag and a 20ish strawberry blonde.

I don't meet anyone's eyes—it's engaging.

Good, two spots at the bar at the far end.

I walk quickly to sit on one chair and put my purse on the other.

The bartender spots me and holds up a bottle of vodka in questioning way.

Everyone drinks vodka. At least, I don't have to use sign language to order.

"Da, spasibo," I say as he pours my shot.

I grab money from my purse, knowing that it would be more than enough to pay for the shot, and put it on the bar. The bartender grabs the money, smiles and walks away. I hover over my drink hoping to be left alone.

"Boo!" Ethan walks up behind me and puts his arms around my shoulders.

"You, jerk!" I spin around and fist his shoulder.

"Love you, honey," he says as he cups my face and kisses me sweetly on the lips.

Then, he sits down beside me

"Do me a favor. Just nod yes to the vodka," I whisper.

"Here he comes."

The bartender approaches with raised eyebrows and a broad smile to offer the bottle of vodka to Ethan.

"*Nyet.*"

I turn and roll my eyes.

"Vodka and …" he points to the tonic.

"Ahhh…" the bartender answers with apparent understanding.

Ethan takes the shot from me, pours it in his glass of tonic, and stirs. Then, he points at the straws.

"Now, we can share a drink that we really like," he announces, gloating.

"Very cute, smarty pants," I grin.

"Now, what were we talking about?" He says as he leans into my space and thumps my chandelier earring.

Something catches my eye—I glance around to see six men dressed in green military garb rush into the bar with machine guns held waist level.

What the hell! My jaw drops in shock.

Ethan spins around on the bar stool and mirrors my surprise.

"Everyone—up against the wall!" the first man shouts in Russian. The man is short and muscular with long black hair which he'd pulled back in a pony tail.

Not understanding what he said, we watch everyone else.

Then, we rush to comply—backs to the wall.

Glad I left my purse at the bar. I won't draw attention to myself at least.

The leader, a tall guy in his late 20's with sandy blonde hair and dark brown vacant eyes, pulls the slide back on his weapon and smiles.

Good God, look at his face! Half of his face is tattooed with another face—an older version of his face. How weird is that?

The others fan out in the room—looking at the faces against the wall.

What do they want? This same thing actually happened in Texas at a small town honky tonk with my parents in tow, only uniformed local cops were taking command. My purse was left on the table. They searched everyone. They were looking for a face and drugs, a stash of drugs. Guess that explained the lack of search warrants. They claimed a big drug deal was in process at the bar.

These commandos aren't searching for property. They study faces looking for someone in particular. They pat down the guys for guns. The leader and another man pat down only the women, moving from the center of the room to the end. These are guys with swagger and big egos, the kind of guys that usually notice me. I grimace at the thought.

I grab Ethan's hand, squeeze it lightly and let it drop.

I hope he doesn't talk to me or ask me a question. I can't flare in anger about this crap. Women are forced into prostitution all the time here. They could easily whisk me out of here without leaving a trace. Unfortunately, Russia is like a big frat party with no consequences.

I grit my teeth, and my jaw flexes in fury.

I watch the cold dark eyes, the eyes of a snake, study the face of the strawberry blonde. Then, he scans the length of her body several times slowly. He moves his face closer to hers—his diamond earring glittering as he cocks his head sideways.

The more he looks the more interested he becomes. Her green eyes open widely and her eyebrows knit together.

The shift, the twinkle in his eyes, reveals a more than necessary interest.

Gag!

He leans into her space one arm supporting his body as he inches toward her face.

Her lips purse. Her eyes become fierce, and she stands taller.

He stands upright and thrusts his hand roughly under her armpit and leisurely moves it along the outside of her turtleneck sweater along her curvy waist.

"Hmmmm…" he smiles.

Yea, so much more than necessary. Go to a happy place and block this out! Don't give him the satisfaction of making you squirm. He loves control. Don't make him assert control! It'll probably make him more excited. Don't react and cause more problems for yourself!

He grazes the back of his hand across her midriff along her pant line. He seems to be lost in his thoughts.

He grabs her shoulders and spins her to face the wall. He once again runs his hands slowly from her armpits to her pant line. Then, he moves his hands down her legs and then puts them on her hips. He squeezes her buttocks hard—laughing darkly with satisfaction.

My heart tries to hammer a hole out of my chest. I stand rigid with my hands balled up in fists at my sides, gritting my teeth.

He presses his body against hers covering it with his. He dry humps her a couple of times and pulls her sweater up to feel her creamy skin, kneading his hands along the flat of her lower back and waist. Suddenly, he grabs her wrists and pulls her lower torso back toward his body—pushing her wrists and hands onto the wall as if he is going to frisk her.

I'd like to take that machine gun to shoot off his penis and stuff it in his mouth!

I hear him breathing hard as he grabs her waist with one hand and claws at her turtle neck collar with the other. He bites her neck hard as she screams "No!" Ignoring her, he moves his hands from the back to the front of her sweater, clawing upward under her bra and grabbing her breasts roughly, squeezing, biting and dry humping her. He makes sucking sounds as he nestles into her neck. I see him open his mouth wide and bite into her skin over and over again. The blood begins to ooze out as he uses his teeth with more force. He moves his hand to her midriff and savagely forces it down the front of her pants—busting the button and zipper.

She jerks toward the wall and shrieks. With an easy smile and a pause to glance around, he moves his hand to the back of her pants and pushes them down.

He steps back to look at her exposed bikini panties, his head tilting in a vertical stare of evaluation. With lightning speed, he produces a switchblade and moves in close behind her—brushing against her while whispering in her ear.

Pushing then holding her sweater up, he traces her spine in a zig zag pattern from top to bottom with the point of blade. From the side, I can see tears well up in her eyes as she prepares to be stabbed. Then, in a flash, he lets the sweater fall and tears through one side of her underwear with the knife then the other. He tosses them aside with a chuckle and pushes her head into the wall while pulling her waist to his body. He unzips his fly and shoves his body into hers with a grunt of nauseating satisfaction.

I'd like to take that knife and shove it up his ass! I look away in disgust. My teeth are grinding and my nails are digging into my clenched fists.

I hear the scream of another woman who is being manhandled in the room –it's the bleached blonde with the Louis Vuitton purse.

Oh, no! What is this—commando orgy?

My heart races and my palms sweat as I stand like a mannequin, frozen in fear of being noticed.

I continue to watch, a captive audience member not wanting to draw any additional attention to myself.

I watch with nausea as she looks away from the leader's groaning face chewing on her neck—suckling on the control, the power and the blood. She stares blankly at the entrance of the bar. Her eyes look dull and blank. Her jaw is clenched and rigid.

I scream silently as my thoughts race.

Chunks of her soul being torn away by that parasite! Her eyes tell everything. Maybe, she's holding out hope for help. If she looks at the entrance, she doesn't have to see the horror in the faces around her. I hope she survives. I hope all of us survive.

I look down at the floor to break from the tragic scene. Then, I glance at Ethan quickly. He is transfixed in disbelief.

One of the men calls to him. Even more startled, I glance around. The man with the pony tail smiles broadly and speaks in broken English, for the benefit of Americans in this popular tourist hotel.

"You enjoying the slut, Mikhail? Will you have her once or twice? Maybe, we all try her. She looks like she taste good," he smiles again, a dirty lustful smile.

The leader humps her harder and laughs loudly. He holds up two fingers in response and thrusts his body into hers again.

"Twice is good. The second time-no clothes and more blood. Everyone gets to stop and watch," the militiaman translates with a wink.

I turn my head away in revulsion, choosing to look at the floor as I rotate my body.

I saw a documentary about violent crimes – one young virgin in the 1930's lured by a man onto a train under the pretense of a date. He sexually attacked her–gnawing and biting her naked skin. She eventually died from the wounds… and that was before HIV.

She should pee or fart, something to disrupt his savage train of thought.

Think—rain, shower or dripping faucet.

His humping abruptly stops, and he grunts in pleasure.

"Mikhail! Another tall man with short-cropped red hair crosses the room toward him. He drags along a dark-haired panicked man, stymied by a strangle hold. He angles his machine gun into the man's portly belly.

"Let's go! We're finished," another militiaman apparently shouts.

I venture a look around.

Across the room, the screaming woman, a willowy tall blonde with ice blue eyes, stops screaming. Her attacker shoves his forearm under her throat—muffling her screams. He unzips her pants. His switchblade positioned near her face. I stare in abject terror.

His face! It looks like someone sliced it…. from the top of his right check across his lips to the bottom of his left jaw. One long jagged gash severing lips which healed—unevenly.

I swallow the "potato' wedged in my throat.

In one swift move, the blade easily tears through the line of buttons on her scoop necked sweater. The other men notice the scene, watching with glistening hungry eyes. A few lick their lips in expectation like hyenas at a kill.

I slowly cast my eyes back at the leader.

Please let this be the end of it all. If he goes, they'll follow.

"*Da*!!" The leader snickers looking down at his pants which had fallen around his ankles. He grabs the girl by the waist to position her in front of him. He pulls her blood-caked blonde hair aside and yanks her collar down to show-off her bubbling neck wound on the right side. He licks the wound from collarbone to earlobe— licking it like an ice cream cone. His hand then goes under her sweater and slides under her bra groping for her left breast. He grabs it tightly like a tug of war rope. His hand balls up under the sweater as he digs his nails into her breast deeply, holding her in place. He groans loudly in satisfaction. Laughter fills the room as the group revels in their leader's joy. He smiles broadly—his mouth and lips smeared with her blood.

Schadenfreude! What a surprise! Barf!!! Maybe, he won't kill her since his task is complete. Maybe, he'll just go. Maybe, it ends now. I think as I shudder.

I hear a loud slap and turn to look. The disfigured man shoves the willowy blonde against the wall. She turns her face to one side and touches her right check. Tears roll down her face. Her face contorts in horror.

"Give her something to remember you by, Artur" the man with the pony tail shouts in Russian. He glares at me with bloodshot dark blue eyes—translating with a twisted smile.

"Hmmm…" He puts away his knife and jerks the woman by the wrist away from the wall. In an instant, he spins her around so she faces him. He clamps his forearm across her throat and grabs his switchblade. With one quick movement, he arcs the blade above her left breast and into her cleavage stopping just below her right breast. The blood begins to seep from the cut. He jerks her around to face him and tilts his head to one side to examine his work. She shrieks and cris crosses her arms protectively against her chest. She crumples to the floor in a heap crying louder. He nudges her onto her stomach with his boot, unzips his pants and straddles her. He pulls down her pants to continue. He grabs her hair with one hand—pulling her head back to center her. Her arms and elbows follow her hair backward and he plunges himself into her. She screams in torment while he heaves and thrusts to the sound of the applause in the room. I look away, my body quaking with fear.

He repositions himself and continues to pump her furiously while the men whistle and jeer.

"Ah…" He smiles broadly, stops and pulls away from her

The faint smell of bleach, of his fluids, fills the air.

"Please leave me alone," she cries as she hunches over the floor face down. Ponytail translates mimicking her emotion. He moves in closer to get a better look.

That heartless bastard! If he didn't terrify me, I'd try to kill him!

"One more thing," Artur sneers as pushes her down and he rolls onto her again.

He flashes his gleaming blade to the onlookers as he shoves her into the floor—waving it above her head.

"Please don't hurt me anymore!" She sobs uncontrollably. Ponytail mocks her and rubs his eyes as if crying.

She cranes her neck to look at him. Her eyes widen in horror at the sight of the blade.

"Please I beg you," she pleads. He translates and clasps his hands together as if begging.

He draws back his fist and punches her hard in the side of the face.

She lay unconscious on the floor.

I turn to look away and tilt my head down.

He stares for a few seconds at her left buttock and then pushes the blade into the top of her left hip like he is writing with a pen—carving into her skin.

I shake uncontrollably at the sight of this woman's nightmare.

"Something to remember me by—my initials," Artur chuckles as he stands up and pulls up his pants. More whistling, applause and a flutter of high fives as the men walk past him to look at the woman on the floor, a prized trophy at a major sporting event.

Ponytail takes great pleasure in providing an English translation to the group as he stares at me.

Poor woman. They have their target. They should leave. This blood lust should end now. I could be next.... This is just a spectacle of sadism and sex. Is it over?

A glacial shiver races down my spine.

Ethan! He sees all of this and he can't do anything to protect me!

I glance quickly over at him. A militiaman points a gun at his head. He obviously noticed our interaction as a couple.

I shouldn't have grabbed his hand to comfort him! The sour milk taste of guilt floods my mouth and stomach.

As Ethan looks at me with helpless horror, Ponytail suddenly moves toward me—lunging forward and grabbing my arm.

A tree of flaming anger burns through every appendage in my body.

Chapter 12

I grit my teeth. I pull back; then, I allow Ponytail to pull me forward and bring my cowboy boot down hard on his right instep. Taking my left hand, I ram it up to his nose. He releases me, falls backward onto the floor and moans in agony—the perfect opportunity to kick him between the legs.

I draw back my leg back as quickly as possible and kick him in the crotch with turbine force.

Make him hurt! It's payback time for me and those women!

He grabs his genitals as the team stands stupefied, mouths agape.

"You bitch! I'll make an example of you!"

I look up at Ethan and at the weapon aimed at his head. Ethan stares in wide-eyed shock. My eyes dart from Ethan to the weapon and back again to Ethan. His eyes sparkle in recognition.

I've created the distraction that no one expected.

Now, Ethan! Don't stand down! His comrades expect him to win!! They'll stand down to watch him win to watch him deal with me, the woman who shamed him!! Use that!! Be a surprise to him!! He reads people. He doesn't consider you a threat!

"Now!" I mouth—my eyes bullets of motivation.

Ethan violently elbows the man next to him in the stomach, creating a diversion to grab his weapon, stepping behind him to aim his gun at Mikhail. Ethan's face is taut as he stares with deadly intent.

Suddenly, Ponytail lunges toward my ankle and latches on to it while reaching for the other.

In an instant, I become a bargaining chip—leverage in a fire fight.

"You don't realize I wear a … How you call it? A cup." He cackles with satisfaction as a blood-curdling smile plays on his lips.

He laughs as I struggle to free myself. He's pulling himself toward me.

"Ethan! Help! Do something!" I beg.

I look at him in horror, wondering if he'll step up. In one quick move, Ponytail grabs my other ankle, forcing me down to the floor. With a *thud*, all air evacuates from my lungs.

His mouth curls in a twisted dark smile as I lie momentarily stunned.

"My example" he announces huskily as he reels me in flipping me over to face him. My fists pound him furiously fueled by hate and rage, a fiery torch of searing self-righteousness pitted against a tsunami of evil.

Ethan, you love me. Don't let this happen! I'll hate you forever if you don't protect me!

"Yes, this is going to be fun," he smiles. I turn my head to the side, and he grabs my face with both hands and covers my mouth with his—his tongue pushing into my throat.

As I punch and squirm, he chuckles. He keeps his mouth trained on mine—pressing into me.

I move my knee ever so slightly. It's not in position.

With his thumbs, his hooks his hands on either side of my hips—pulling my pants down and forcing his tongue down my throat repeatedly. My blood congeals and my heart pumps wildly. I continue to wiggle and punch.

Stay chilled! You'll find your moment and maybe Ethan will find his resolve.

The cold air hits me below the waist like a gust of wind. I tremble involuntarily.

Ponytail suddenly releases me and laughs. I scowl at him in disgust and lie still.

"You want to see me rape your wife? Everybody watch me rape your wife. And you'll watch them rape your wife because you are coward."

I'll die before I let that happen. They'll have to kill me first. Ethan knows that about me. I'm a fighter. I love you Ethan, but I despise you for letting this go this far. I may well die before you figure out what to do. I think Ponytail may be trying to goad you into action with a new target to save Mikhail.

Ponytail turns back to me with an eager smile, grabbing my battering arms. He pins my wrist above my head with one hand and licks the side of face. Using the other hand he claws at my top until my breast is exposed. With a gleam in his eyes, he moves his head to my breast and suckles it loudly while watching my expression.

What's that on his hand? It's a ring—a ring on his left hand. He's married! The psycho bastard is married to some poor woman! My level of repulsion just hit a new level, dangerous to my control and focus.

"You disgust me!" I shout as I buck up underneath him.

I catch a glimpse of Ethan in my periphery. He's biting his lip. I'm surrounded by an audience of lascivious cheering men.

"I like disgust. I want more disgust from you!" he cackles.

He returns his mouth to my breast—nibbling it and rubbing his free hand back and forth on my crotch. I look to the left and notice a guy dressed in black like the others, but he's wearing dress boots instead of military boots. I stare at his shoes, disconnecting from the moment.

The stays are pulled tight across the front with a buckle across the top. And there are... parallel pink and yellow squiggly lines drawn across the toe. A smiley face stares at me from inside the instep.

I'd bet a kid drew those squiggles. Ewwww!... I bet he's a Dad—Mafioso/counterfeit cop by day and daddy-o at night.

A glowing cherry ash of a cigarette butt falls next to his boot as he cheers on Ponytail—his fist raised, his hips thrusting forward and his gun lowered.

Da! More! Yeah! Go!

My around-the-knees pants trap my legs. Ponytail is breathing heavily, in full arousal mode. Leaning into me and groaning. We gnarl together like trees, one struggling to survive in the shadow of another.

My resistance increases his libido. I need to disconnect and be lifeless.

I look in to his eyes for a moment, they're dark and glittery like a hyena's at a kill. He pauses and smiles as he looks towards Ethan.

"She's very responsive—your wife. Her body so tight and sexy. I make her groan in pleasure so you can hear her disgust. Everyone else hear her too." Ponytail returns his hand to my crotch and his head to my breast, nibbling and suckling loudly. His fingers begin to explore aggressively rhythmically, and my breathing changes. He pauses and looks at me, grinning.

"*Da*, that's what I want. You ready for me," he chuckles as I grimace. I flex my knees to check his position and squirm to escape his continual assault.

This is self-loathing and disgust. My body likes this, but my mind hates it. I like for Ethan to dominate me, on my terms. I feel safe then, but now I'm a prisoner of my biology. Now, my surgically-repaired anatomy betrays me. Rancid revulsion roots in my throat like dangerous debris—threatening to damn the stream of life-saving thoughts. He raises his boot between my legs and pushes my pants down to my ankles.

"You still can't go anywhere. Does your husband usually fuck you like this?" he says loudly, looking around the room with a smirk. He releases my wrists and pushes me onto my side. His right forearm locks around my neck. He spoons me, panting and forcing his fingers inside one orifice then another.

The guys roar as I seethe with hate. The laughter and applause anchor my resolve to kill him somehow.

"Yes, I have fun—great fun with your body. It's soft and it want me."

Retracting my neck back, I lash forward like a snake to bite his forearm. The taste of blood and flesh in my mouth never welcomed until now.

"Fuck! You stupid kunt! Accept your fate as my prize!" He says as he shoves me away to inspect his now bleeding arm.

Time is what I need—time to think and time to do.

Balancing with my elbows on my belly, I check his location. He's slowly crawling toward me on all fours like a lion stalking a crippled gazelle. With a smirk, he pauses, resting on one side to unzip his pants. I use the moment to look away from him.

I need to find something to disrupt his thoughts, to thwart his actions.

Maybe, a cocktail stir stick, a knife or a pen.

I crawl across the floor toward leather shoes before he grabs my ankle. Fisting my hands, digging my elbows, knees and toes into the floor, I resist the only way I can.

I glance around to see him on all fours, ready to penetrate me. A loud laugh escapes his lips as he pulls me toward him.

He grabs my hair pulling my head back as I feel the touch of his naked thigh. His large hand pushes on the small of my back forcing my back to arch and my hips to pop up.

Oh, no. Please no! The point of no return! Ethan, where are you? If this happens, we're done!

I feel his nakedness angling close, his leg and chest hair grazing my skin, as he positions himself behind me on all fours.

"Now, the way I fuck is different. It's rough, "he explains to the group as a professor might explain a lesson to a class—a class of militiamen with guns lowered enjoying today's entertainment, today's "show".

"There are more opportunities for...um. How you say?... Pleasure—here." He cups my bottom, squeezing it hard digging in his fingers and grunting. His head and neck wrap over my shoulder like a snake and his mouth latches onto my neck, sucking and bruising like a leech. He pauses, exhales deeply and props his torso against me, like a runner leaning against a wall catching his breath and collecting his thoughts before a race. His biting aftershave assaults my nostrils—the mix of cedar and lime both numbing and repellant. It carries me to a higher level of unknown misery.

I can't calm myself with deep breathing without inhaling that scent. I'm allergic to Cedar. My resolve is tittering, unbalanced and weakening by the minute. Must hold on with shallow breaths.

"One last thing... that makes it so good for me. I like to hear the woman scream," he says hoarsely.

The audience cheers and hollers—the "show" just got better. Their guns hang by their sides as they await the second act. I hear a *click* and crane my neck around to see a gleaming silver blade.

He's got a knife! He's going to rape me and sodomize me with a knife!

My eyes dart from Ethan to Ponytail and back again suggestively.

Take the shot, Ethan! No indecision, no more time now. Be courageous! Shoot Ponytail. He'll slaughter me with this knife otherwise. Mikhail may try to grab your gun, but you must believe that you can hold on. His men will stand down. After all, Mikhail is an experienced pro and their leader. He has the advantage. And Mikhail's men may shoot at you, but you can use him as a shield. It's your only chance to save me and save your soul! If you live and I don't, you'll be forever changed!

Moments pass—pregnant with the promise of my violent rape and grisly slaughter. An icy spider of fear crawls on my skin, along my neck and on my back.

It's my only chance! Now! Act like his broken bitch, his submissive. He's thinking with his penis anyway. Use that.

Dropping my head to the floor, I see his clutched knife next to my hand. Looking backward beyond the arc of my spread legs, I gently take and stroke his genitals.

"You win. I give-up. Why don't you put yourself in my mouth? You may decide to keep me, not kill me."

He gasps and groans while grabbing my breast and dry humping me. As he positions himself to move into me, I cradle, twist and stab with a pen—burying it in his scrotum.

"Fuck! You kunt! I kill you!" As I wiggle away, he lunges forward grabbing my hair, jerking my head back and forth like the steering wheel of an out-of-control car.

"*Nyet*!! The pain—I can't stand it!" He screams. I fall forward as he pushes me out of the way. Peeking behind as I scramble across the floor on my knees, I see him doubled over in a pool of blood, his teeth gritting in agony as he pulls out the pen. His searing screams so repetitive they seem to echo in the now still room. The cheering stops, the onlookers frozen in disbelief at the sight of their fallen comrade. Staring at Ethan with white hot intensity, I nod. My eyes pleading yet demanding that he take action—resolve over reluctance.

I did it! Not safe yet. Run!

In an instant, Ethan aims and fires at Ponytail's arm and fires again at his legs. Swinging his weapon around, Ethan trains his sights on Mikhail, who's smirking now.

Mikhail motions a man to Ponytail's side. Bleeding, impaled Ponytail rises with help and leans on his comrade to leave the bar.

Mikhail walks to Ethan. His posture is military erect, shoulders back and chest out. Ethan keeps his eye in the scope and tightens his lips.

That guy is walking up to the gun, point blank range close. Don't let him grab the gun, Ethan!

"*Nyet!* No further!' Ethan orders.

Mikhail stops and stares at Ethan, his face contorted in amusement. His eyebrows raised and his eyes dark—two cesspools of cruel thought. He smiles a toothy mocking smile.

With a steely unwavering stare, he raises his hand and wags his finger back and forth at Ethan's face. He pauses for a moment, continuing to stare. The silence is deafening, the screams muffled and the room is hemorrhaging terror. And suddenly, he bursts into laughter.

"You think you win here—no win. We begin play now."

Turning on his heel, he motions his men out of the bar and walks away.

Chapter 13

Bar patrons rush to help the two women while we fall into each other's arms crying.

Ethan draws back and shakes his head as if to fling the tears away. Finally, he wipes them away with the back of his hand. "Are you OK?" he asks me, trying to keep the tremble out of his voice. "You're ice cold."

"You are too." I reach out for his hand again, not ready to let go. Arm in arm, we leave the bar with a bottle of vodka and go to our room. An albatross of ice-cold fear accompanies us down the hallway to our room.

"What a nightmare!! You were a warrior in that bar!!" Ethan says as we lock the door behind us and immediately pour ourselves two shots of vodka. "So aggressive—you changed the outcome! I know it was difficult for you. I'm so sorry you had to go through that," Ethan snarls.

"We changed the outcome," I say downing my shot. "You played as big a role as I did. You should own that." Looking away from him and toward the door, I continue, "I'm so grateful that we're okay, but I'm worried about Mikhail or Ponytail seeking some sort of retribution against us." I utter fearful of my where my thoughts are leading me; so, I down my shot as a form of distraction and pour another.

"We have to tell Natasha and ask what precautions to take. We just have to be a little more careful that's all," he says, avoiding my eyes—choosing to converse with the curtains in the room.

"I'm not sure that that plan is air-tight. We don't know who these people are. One thing for sure—Natasha will be explosive when we tell her. She'll bind us to chairs in the room for the rest of the trip and we probably should be," I mutter.

"I wish I could've helped you more, prevented that all together," Ethan says as he lowers his eyes to the floor.

"You did help by not being a hot head. You didn't get hurt or killed, and you didn't make my problems worse. It made the scene easier to cope with," I say while guiding his chin upward so that I can look him square in the eyes. I kiss him lightly, and he pushes me away.

"Here, have a shot and a hot bath. I'll set it up for you," he suggests, eager to help.

"I probably need a rabies shot and a few sessions of therapy after being around those feral dogs," I say to make him smile.

Cruel sick men who lust for power and blood as much as sex.

I wrap my arms around my upper body and hug myself in quiet appreciation of being spared. My eyes burn with tears which spill over as I step into the steamy hot bath, park myself and grab the bottle of vodka—uncapping it and tipping it upward for a big gulp. My eyes burn as the fire claws down my throat and into my stomach, radiating towards my extremities. I cough and sink lower and lower into the hot tub as the slap of naked truth hits me again and again.

What an awful scene—a test of composure, strength and survival. How did I manage to handle it the way I did? I think I have to give credit to horses. My riding misadventure with Luke really helped me tonight. I'd have fallen to pieces if I hadn't experienced that! It taught me to leverage my instincts, to think powerful and be powerful. It taught me that I'm tougher than I ever dared to imagine. It could have been so much worse. Those women could have died. I could have died or been gang raped or both. Both of us could've died... And I'll see a therapist to erase those bloodthirsty sickos from my mind. Ethan will probably need a dose of that too.

***

I turn to look at the clock—6 am. I shift onto my left side to snuggle into Ethan's back.

"Are you awake too?" he asks softly as he rotates toward me.

"I don't want to ever go back to that place! The sooner we put that behind us the better." I say, shuddering.

"No arguments here. And we can't tell Natasha," Ethan says lovingly, stroking my hair as he talks.

Natasha was smart to keep us under house arrest. Now, look at the mess we're in, scared to go and scared to stay, scared to talk to her since she may think it's too dangerous to continue.

"Don't you think we should tell her a diluted version of what happened and leave tonight? Then, we can return in a few days to try to go forward with the adoption. I'm certain they will search for us. Maybe, that'll throw them off track. We don't want our baby to be a target too," I say as my eyes begin to mist.

We're now the hunted. We don't know who those people were. They may have to power to destroy our adoption plans.

The tears spill onto my cheeks.

"Look, we shouldn't leave tonight. They probably expect us to try to rush out of here. We act calm, we look normal, we stay on plan. We'll tell Natasha soon; so, she can help us protect the baby. It'll be more difficult to avoid capture the longer we stay. We need to grab our son and leave as soon as possible. "

"What now? What can we do now to fill our time? Safely? We can't just sit in here and do nothing. I don't want to spend my time worrying about what can happen."

"You're right. The way I see it we're safer in a public place than cornered like mice in a hotel room. We need some distraction. Let's start with breakfast. Let's go to the front desk and ask about the breakfast hours. Casually, we should mention we heard gunfire coming from the bar that way we may be able to find out who those men are," Ethan suggests.

I'm ambivalent about that, want to know but afraid to know.

Oily dread starts to pool in my throat as I think about the possibilities, either way it's bad news, Mafia or bounty hunters or public officials.

"Great idea! I'll ask the front desk on the way to the hotel restaurant," I offer insincerely.

At least, I'll avoid Ethan's edited version of the answers if I ask the questions.

A tall 20ish something blonde with green eyes mans the front desk of the hotel.

She peers up at me as I walk toward her and turns her eyes back to the sheaf of papers in her hand.

"Excuse me, will you please tell me the restaurant hours for breakfast?"

"Yes, the hours are 8 am until 10 am every morning. Do you require the lunch hours or a menu?"

"No, *Spasibo.* By the way, we heard gunshots last night when we walked in the lobby. I think they came from the bar. What happened?" I asked, my eyebrows raised, knitted in counterfeit curiosity.

Anna, Ms. Front Desk, stares intently at me, her mouth a knotted line that doesn't want to move. She checks the sides of her desk with her peripheral vision, never moving her head.

"Why do you care to know?" she asks pointedly.

"Well, I'm wondering if we should be worried for our safety. Should we?"

Anna now frowning in irritation nods her head "no" in response. She punctuates her response by rolling her eyes.

I hold her gaze, knowing she may say more if I'm patient. I stand and wait, my arms crossed over my chest.

"Do not worry. You are safe. The Chief of Police and his men search for someone last night. They found the man. The shots fired were required to make him follow orders. It's nothing unusual," she says coolly.

I swallow hard as the information fills my brain with fear. I cough as if my head is being held under water. I'm drowning in scary thoughts, molten hot panic races through my veins. I cough again, gasping for air. My heart is battering the underside of my chest. My face feels hot as it reddens. My clothes feel suddenly uncomfortable as if I'm wearing itchy wool. I push my hair aside and massage the back of my now stiff itchy neck.

"Do you require water?" Anna asks with an iceberg stare.

"*Nyet, I'll be okay. Spasibo.* " I amble away striking my right fist against my chest to be more convincing to Anna.

Oh my God! Ethan shot a deputy—an ordained police officer. Oh my God, they're totally corrupt and amoral! They have the intelligence and resources to get us. And the adoption! I feel my blood run cold. Has this ruined everything? My worried eyes find Ethan across the room; he's standing patiently with his arms resting at his sides. As he reads my expression, his smile fades into a frown. I walk toward him and stand beside him, not wanting to see him process the implications of the bad news.

Grabbing my arm, he faces me, staring into my eyes with blowtorch intensity.

"Tell me everything," he demands.

Chapter 14

"Not here," I say, gesturing for him to follow me to the breakfast bar. I need to think, and I'm hungry. We'll discuss this in our room after breakfast."

"No," he says. "I want to know now. I need to know."

I study his eyes. They are piercing, hard and angry.

"We have to act normal," I tell him calmly. "No theatrics from you. No tears from me. Especially now."

I see the Ultimate Fighter look in his eyes, ready to take a beating but ready to exact some payback too. He wants to deny the truth. And he needs to process it, to digest it. He needs this time.

"So, what's for breakfast this morning?" I ask as Ethan and I peer over the possibilities, all lined up along both sides of a steam table set-up.

"Let's see we have—sliced tomatoes, coleslaw, hard boiled eggs, cold cuts and porridge," he says with a frown.

My stomach somersaults backward at the sight of food.

What about crunchy grainy cereal, bagels, or scrambled eggs? Porridge is the closest thing to oatmeal that I can find and tolerate at this time of day.

And so it is porridge, probably every damn day.

Ethan swallows a bite of a cold cut and mustard sandwich while looking at the choices of the other patrons.

"The blonde at the front desk—she's walking toward us," he says suddenly.

What does she want? Did she notice my nervousness?

We lock eyes, promising one another to swallow our angst.

"Did you find all that you require?" she asks Ethan with a half smile.

"*Da, Spasibo.* Love it!" Ethan answers sincerely.

She holds his gaze for a minute or two and turns her attention to me.

She looks at me in a challenging way.

Really, I hate these choices, but it's all I care to shove down my throat.

"This is the best porridge I've ever tasted, but how about some fresh honey dew melon?"

"What is it—honey dew?" she asks suddenly interested.

"It's fruit. Just wish there was some fresh fruit."

She laughs loudly, slapping the table with her hand.

"Fresh fruit in Russia in the winter. That is so funny! There are many things available in Russia, some good and some bad, compared to your country. For example, peace and comfort here come with a price, follow the rules or face the bad result. In the United States, follow the rules or your government slaps your hand after the court decides it can. We are different. If you do not notice, the bad result is quick here." She smiles in a small knowing way as she tilts his nose upward. She leans closer in to tell us more. Long curled blood red nails accent her vein-rich hand which rests on the table. Her cuticles dangle multiple hangnails.

"The police always find the best way to produce the result to hurt the most," she announces as she strikes her hand on the tablecloth like a gavel.

She suspects something about us. I bet she's an informant.

"*Spasibo,* we pride ourselves on following the rules, especially in countries with less freedoms than ours," Ethan counters with a cool smile.

Anna puts her hands on hips, standing instantly taller. Her lips knot as her chin tilts upward, her eyes looking down at us now.

"Well, I am on break to take coffee now. Good bye."

And with that, Anna spins on her heel, heading to the coffee urn.

"Put everything out of your head. We linger and act normal. Be playful," Ethan orders in a whispery voice.

He's right. She wants to rattle us. I won't give her the satisfaction!

"Hey, I know why breakfast is not as social as lunch or dinner," I declare.

A smile starts to cross his face.

"Why would that be?" He asks curiously, his smile growing bigger. His eyebrows rise in curious interest.

"Because no one feels talkative when they're trying to choke down food that they don't enjoy. They're probably hungry and want to forget what they ate breakfast," I lean back and cross my arms and angle my chin up, proud of my deduction.

"Well, I'm glad that you've got this all figured out. I'm sure people will be thrilled to hear your explanation" He flashes a bright smile and turns away to track Anna.

"As a matter of fact, I bet they will," I say as I tear the corner of a paper napkin and wad it up between my fingers. He's too busy trying to disguise his amusement and control his laughter to notice what I'm doing. I thump my little wad of paper at his head and smile.

Anna walks by our table with her steamy cup of coffee. She sits at the table closest to ours.

"I don't have any answers yet. This is complex. I don't think we should hide like mice, hiding from the cat. Natasha will force us to do that if we tell her. She may shut down the whole process if we tell her. Remember she warned us about complications. We stay on plan, but very cautiously."

I accept that—there's no easy answer. We can't run because Natasha would want to know why, and we can't tell Natasha. So, to be able to complete the adoption, we have to avoid capture by the police and avoid telling Natasha about our problem, even though she's the one who can really help us.

***

"It surprises me that there are so many vodka bars everywhere. It reminds me of the hot dog and pizza vendors in Times Square. And they're so busy at lunchtime," I comment the day after breakfast with Anna.

"I can't imagine drinking a shot or two of vodka during my lunch hour and going back to work at the bank. That would be scary in a lot of different ways."

"Did you notice that there are one or two "community" glasses? And the glass moves from one customer to the next without being washed? Proving my point about sharing vodka—it's germ-free and guilt-free. After all, it's alcohol."

"Hey, why don't we have red caviar and sturgeon for lunch and go to a vodka bar afterwards? I'm curious to look around after what Natasha told us about them."

"We'll ask Natasha if it's safe."

How ironic! We'll ask Natasha if it's safe to go to the vodka bar, but we won't ask if we're in danger of being slaughtered or kidnapped by the police.

I stare down at my next spoonful of lumpy white mush for a few seconds.

"Do you think we should tell her now?" I ask.

"No, I really don't. We just always need to be aware of the fact that we have to think and re-think our every outside-the-room decision."

That means no vodka bar. Guess will make dinner an eating adventure. I'll probably balloon up by 30 pounds while we're here.

Dinner is short for dinner party—a meal lasting several hours with several courses segmented by shots of vodka. A carafe or two of vodka sits in the middle of the table, displacing a flower arrangement or candles, for easy pouring. The last course consists of a box of Russian chocolates and hot tea. And the Russian chocolates are irresistible—treasures for the tongue and bounty for the brain.

Ethan enjoys the vodka tradition a lot and tries to heed Dad's warning:

"Don't trade shots with the Russians. They'll drink you under the table. Vodka consumption here is about 28 bottles annually for every man, woman and child. I know you think you can drink and hold your own, but don't go there. Sip your shot. Drink the toast shot or two, then, call it quits for the night."

Gosh, I hope Mr. Party Boy can follow that advice.

Chapter 15

We're sleeping soundly in our hotel room when a knock at the door followed by loud banging awakens us. I glance at the clock on the nightstand—it's 7 am— and the sky outside is still pitch black. Ethan jumps up and dashes to the door.

"Who's there?" He asks angrily while I sit up in bed, clutching the covers around my neck.

My thoughts, once raked into an organized pile, travel like fallen leaves on a windy day.

Can it be Mikhail? Oh, God, we don't have the gun beside the bed. I fling off the covers, grab the gun, hidden behind the ironing board in the closet, stash it under the covers and climb back into bed.

"Natasha. Open door," she answers tersely.

What's going on? Why is she here at 7 am in the morning? Could she have heard about the bar?

Natasha, dressed in designer finery and cloaked in mink, rushes into the room followed by two confused strangers. For once, Natasha's eyes show fear like a deer discovered. Without a word of greeting or explanation, she begins speaking Russian to the women, one tall and one short, who enter the room.

Who are these people? What's going on here? I vault out of bed, thankful to be wearing pajamas.

Ethan and I stand bleary-eyed and bewildered in our untidy room. A pile of dirty clothes lies in a corner and the remnants of an unfinished meal rests on the dresser. The white room adorned with grey curtains, one light oak triple dresser and queen bed flanked by two nightstands, seems no worse for the wear. A faded paper print of a winter scene hangs over the bed, a nod to bus station charm with a luxury price tag.

Why didn't Natasha explain or introduce us to these people? It's obvious the way they're talking that they're arguing. We shouldn't just stand here, doing nothing. Ethan begins picking up dirty towels, and I start tidying up around our suitcase.

Then, without a smile or a word of explanation or even an introduction, the group hurries out of the room. Natasha slams the door as the last one out.

What's this about? Who are those people? Why bring them here? Why were they arguing?

We try for several hours to reach Natasha, but she doesn't answer our calls. After breakfast, we lay in bed "watching" TV, a "permissible" activity.

"Well, obviously, it was adoption-related," Ethan remarks with a frown.

"It was almost like a spur-of-the-moment inspection, but it was too brief. And they only debated. There was no interaction with us," I add, looking out toward the window.

Unspoken mental gymnastics overpower all senses—a somersault of what ifs and cartwheels of what went wrong, a handstand onto the balance beam of success or failure and fast spins on the uneven bars of what to do next. Shrill, noxious silence feeds our frustration. Our swollen hearts and tired bodies increasingly ache for closure. A ringing phone forces us back to the confines of the room.

"You meet me for lunch today for adoption officials talk to you."

"What happened this morning?" I ask, gritting my teeth. "Were *they* the people we'll meet with? Why were you arguing?"

"No questions. You know what you need know, the restaurant around the corner at 2 today for lunch. We pick you up and drive you there at 1:45."

I hear the click of the phone as she finishes her sentence.

Yes, we know only what we have to know… Got that loud and clear.

What's scarier—what you know or what you don't?

Chapter 16

"Well, it's time to be judged as good people and worthy parents or not," I remark as I glance anxiously at the clock, the face of which reflects the smears of a quick swipe with a washcloth. The untidy room is now completely clean and organized, one of the things we do to satiate our mutual need for instant gratification and some semblance of control.

Ethan paces repeatedly across the floor, with metronome-like rhythm.

"What could they be looking for or at? Natasha didn't coach us at all." I cross my arms and stare at Ethan.

"All we can do is be ourselves and hope that's good enough." Ethan stops pacing to look into my eyes. I can't help but notice that he's wringing his hands.

"Are you worried like me that Mikhail may crash our meeting or be working behind the scenes to sabotage our efforts?" I ask with a frown.

"Can we possibly do anything different than follow the plan at this point?" he answers glibly as he takes my hand, leading me out the door.

The ice cube burn of the cold weather follows us into the quiet space. I shiver from cold and the importance of the moment.

White walls and square dark wood tables, covered by white tablecloths, positioned closely together fill the room.

A rainbow of igloo colors—white black and brown—fill the room. Thank goodness for a sunlit day. Sunlight from many oblong windows adds warmth and more heat to an area devoid of artwork, plants and color. Displaying our brightest smiles, we greet our examiners as Viktoria shadows us to translate our thoughts. The penetrating stare that we expect upon introduction does not occur; instead, both officials gaze quickly at us and look away. As the waitress begins to cover the table with caviar and other expensive foods, a tall, thin woman with black hair, Yvegeniya, leans forward and begins to ask questions.

"'How many people are in your family? Do you have other children?'"

"'How close does your family live to your home?'"

"'Are you …?'" She makes the sign of the cross in the air and looks at Viktoria.

"'Are you Catholic?'" Viktoria translates.

"We're Christians, but we aren't Catholic," I reply evenly.

Viktoria translates the reply and waits patiently.

What's wrong with this picture? I study her body language. *She might as well be rehearsing a speech. She's very disconnected. She's looking beyond us even when questions are being asked and answered. Meanwhile, her short, large, sullen companion, Svetlana, watches disinterestedly while she chews. We may as well be sparrows resting on the tree branch outside the window, bird-like in importance. We're the interesting diversion to observe while she savors a good meal in a boring situation. A rousing interrogation would be better. At least, they would have to be engaged and committed to conversation.*

Perhaps, due to the Svetlana's obvious boredom and indifference, I notice Viktoria become more animated while conveying lengthy, detailed translations to the simplest of questions.

Hmm…What's so strange? Svetlana is not making eye contact. That's not good.

Yvegeniya is more interested in the whereabouts of the waiter than our answers.

Have we been disqualified? Maybe, there is an interface with the police department.

As the questioning ends, Natasha and Viktoria continue to talk with the officials as we maintain physical invisibility. As if abruptly awakened by the meal just consumed, the brooding Svetlana speaks eagerly, confidently to Natasha and Viktoria.

She has the demeanor of an affected aristocrat dealing with the plowmen.

She glances up and down in our direction and sneers.

Great! Let's not skip the large box of chocolates as you torture us.

This silence makes me dizzy. The meal ends finally. We watch as the Russians exchange good-byes, excluding us from the group.

They don't even acknowledge our presence because we don't exist to them. We aren't really important now. In total silence, we retreat to our room as "breathing wallets"—nothing more, without character, heart or brains.

"Have you ever felt like a chess pawn?"

Ethan looks very serious, his brows knit.

"Have you felt like a chess pawn on a board dotted only with bishops and queens?"

"So much for first impressions. Do you think we made any positive impact?"

"No, but I don't think it matters."

"Why do you think we were made to feel unimportant? Do you think there will be a second meeting? Maybe, there is some bar scene residue tainting this process."

"I hope not. You'd think they wouldn't go to all of this trouble if there was a police mandate. I guess it could be a trick to get money before the process ends."

Even though we received no coaching, it seems unlikely that Viktoria would translate a wrong answer, given the seating arrangement. We sat directly across from the interviewing officials while Natasha faced Viktoria. Natasha positioned herself to be successful with or without our assistance. Several subterranean currents of communication and activity traveled back and forth, never fully revealed to us. It reminded me of my days in middle school as the girl being whispered about while watching, wondering and waiting for a clue.

"Well, after two hours of work, I can tell you that I must meet with women tonight for drinks."

"What did they say about us? What do they think of us? Are we acceptable?" I ask.

"That all for now." *Click*

Give us a bone! Give us some hope!

Did Natasha overlook something again? Did she miss another important step?

"Well, that makes for another sleepless night, "I remark in disgust.

Ethan looks down, shaking his head in disappointment.

Okay, it's a mental marathon tonight, a mental marathon of what ifs.

Chapter 17

The next day, Natasha calls. I move away from the phone so Ethan will answer it. My head aches with "hangover" pain, and I feel very grumpy, not the best time to talk to Natasha.

"What's the latest news? Ethan asks for both of us, his voice laced with barely disguised anger. "What happened at dinner last night?"

There's silence for almost ten seconds. It feels like an eternity.

Finally, Ethan's face lights up. "Are you sure?" He grins with joy, signaling me with a thumbs up. Then, he tells Natasha, "That's great! Thank you!"

Slamming down the phone, he turns to me.

"We're going to the child house!" Before I get the chance to process the news, he grabs me and swings me around by my waist.

"What a relief!" My eyes fill with tears. He holds me close, and I cry on his shoulder, the tears turning to breathless sobs.

Obviously, Mikhail didn't taint that process, but I can't help but think he will intervene at some point. He must know about the adoption, this city is an international adoption hub. He knows Americans travel here for that reason. He probably knows everything about us by now.

I look at Ethan and know why he seems ecstatic and distant.

He's thinking the same thing I am.

"What was the purpose behind the dinner? "I ask later.

"She wouldn't say, but she did say they were sharks."

Given their cold disinterest at lunch, that's not really a surprise. Thank goodness, Natasha is dealing with them.

"Speaking of meals and food, we need to tidy up this room—yesterday's snack food is turning to rock on the dresser, we need another roll of toilet paper, the trash cans are full, and all of the towels are dirty. We've been so caught up in the day-to-day drama, we sort of lost track of our immediate surroundings. Apparently, the maid service doesn't clean the room unless we request it. How odd—huh?" I say as I gaze at our space.

"Maybe, not considering the Mafia presence here. I wouldn't want to know too much or see too much. Would you?" Ethan comments acidly, refusing to meet my eyes.

He's right, of course. I can tell he wonders when the axe hanging over our heads will fall.

"Do you mind looking in the hall for a supply closet? Bet we'd find clean towels and toilet paper in there. You may even want to peek at the inventory in case we need something else."

***

The dawn of a new day, and we venture forth so that I can meet our baby. Before we leave, I take two one hundred dollar bills from my purse fold them in half—putting them at the front of our passport pouch and place it in my top drawer.

Ethan watches me, a look of sudden understanding shadowing his face, and grabs a penny putting it at the left most corner under the pillow on the bed.

For Mikhail, if he or his team searches the room when we're away at any time, we'll have an opportunity to know. Two hundred American dollars may be a temptation to a thief. After all, in third world Russia, there is no middle class—you're either sultan rich or stinking poor. I'll bet these henchmen are desperate. Good grief, doctors here only earn a couple of hundred a month, but the penny may be the perfect trigger wire since it'll move quietly if the mattress is lifted.

With a quick peck, we lock the door and leave.

Our taxi speeds recklessly down the icy two-lane road to our destination. Small, non-descript, makeshift houses and homogeneous multi-story clay or grey apartment buildings monopolize every view. The majority of the homes lack central air and heat and indoor plumbing, as evidenced by the backyard out houses.

Bbbbrrrrrrrr.

I shiver and goose bumps pimple my arms as I picture families gathering wood for heat and using the heat-free outhouse in this killer cold. Snow falls in a way that a torrential rain would, cloaking the entire area white. The car travels farther into the center of town where businesses stand at attention shoulder-to-shoulder lined up along the street like soldiers ready to march in formation. Suddenly, the car veers sharply into an opening between buildings and parks.

The taxi stops, and we step out. I take a moment to look at my surroundings—a large square flanked by an inconspicuous two-story building; in the center of the square, a gated play area peeks from beneath the snow. Dusted with snowflakes, I respectfully travel the icy steps leading to the front door. Once inside, I look left to see an office with a desk, someone sitting at the desk, a couch and a couple of chairs. Straight-ahead just beyond the entry hallway, a staircase rises to the second floor.

A well-dressed attractive tall red head stands up from behind the desk and motions us into her office. Positioned to the right of her desk, a glass display case of toys, arranged like prized awards, catches my eye.

That's unusual. Why put the toys in that case? Maybe, it's a decorative statement.

I'm sure I must appear puzzled. In response, she watches me intently and immediately begins to speak to us in her native language. With the interpreter's help, we formally make our introductions, looking at one another eye-to-eye and shaking hands; then, we sit to talk about the baby. The director's eyes seem to tunnel into my soul to take inventory, her gaze is intense and unwavering. It feels sun lamp hot. She acts both warm and cautious as she should be.

I have nothing to hide. Our intentions are pure and sincere unlike Mikhail. Has he found her and influenced this process? Will I get to meet Dmitry to see what might have been if there was not a Mafia vendetta?

I shudder at the thought of his bloodthirsty violent crew in or near this sanctuary.

As she studies me, I study her, knowing instantly that she cares deeply about the welfare of these children. She is the mother to all of them. And it isn't just a job.

My knees wobble as I think about how she may see me, the real me.

Who am I kidding? I'm not a girly girl. I'm the girl who played in dirt piles, climbed trees, waged war on boys with dirt clods and rocks, captured pollywogs, putting them in my dresser drawers for safekeeping. Poor Mom shrieked at the sight and smell of their rotting bodies when she stored my clean folded clothes in the dresser. I really didn't even like babysitting. I do want to be a Mom desperately. I just hope she thinks that I'm good enough for one of her kids.

Chapter 18

"The child, Dmitry, will be brought to the office in a few minutes," the translator announces. Quickly, unknowingly, I turn away from the translator and walk toward the window. I gaze outside at *the dense, white, patterned art that falls from the sky; how quickly it covers and changes everything within reach!* Awestruck, I feel humbled to be in the company of the small, carefully forged snowflakes. My eyes well with tears of joy.

Now, I'll finally meet my baby. From this day forward, my life changes forever. Thank you for this moment, God.

The enormity of the moment, the tangibility of success, and the long, difficult history to reach this moment send me tumbling over a cliff. Ethan holds me in his arms as my body trembles with the release of months of rigorously controlled emotions.

Facing the doorway as Ethan holds me, I see a nurse carrying a small baby walking toward me. As she gently places him in my arms, my sense of happiness surges like a racehorse breaking from the starting gate, the speed and thrust of thundering hooves not more powerful. My heart is now heavy and full as never before. My eyes well with tears again as I softly kiss his little fuzzy, baldhead and his miniature hands. I rock him and kiss him as everything around us fades to a blur, nothing else matters. Dizzy with emotion, I'm awash in a tidal wave of feelings that I never experienced before in my life, giddiness, intoxication and enchantment. A nod from nature to fulfill a calling, a twist of Fate untwisted—to be a Mom, to be his Mom forever.

After spending time-stopping moments caressing him, I sadly realize that he isn't responding.

Our son, clad in three or four layers of clothing, seems more like a rosy-cheeked baby doll. He's not engaging with me. His chest struggles and rattles each time he uses his lungs!

He's sick! What's wrong with him?

I look up at the translator, my face flush with panic.

"He's sick. What's wrong? Does he have medicine?"

Viktoria rattles off my question and smiles knowingly. "He has a cold. They are treating him. He'll be well soon."

I look at her blankly and him again, looking for signals of discomfort and love. My thoughts run wild.

He's not showing discomfort or irritation with the cold even though he sounds awful. What else can be going on? He's not acting like he dislikes me. He's not pulling away or leaning away. How would I feel if someone I knew put me into a stranger's arms? The nurse didn't let me him to choose to reach for me. She just placed him in my arms. I'll bet he's scared and sick. At times, I act frozen and withdrawn when extremely stressed.

I kiss the top of his head again gently, but don't pull him in for a hug.

This may be the first time he's been showered with unconditional love, warmth and adoration.

You'll get a daily dose of caresses, kisses and love from me, little one—that I promise you. You almost seem stunned by the attention and focus. Your little face looks confused.

Above all, I promise you that you'll know that I love you always and endlessly no matter how long that takes, what it takes. I make that vow here and now.

After ten minutes, the manager signals that the meeting should end now. As the nurse leans toward us, he grasps one of my fingers, using his entire hand, and squeezes. The nurse hoists him up to her shoulder to leave. And as I watch him watch me, his fuzzy little head and beautiful green blue eyes peering over the nurse's shoulder, my eyes mist and spill more tears.

As we prepare to leave, having said our goodbyes, the manager grabs Viktoria's arm and points at us. She speaks excitedly in Russian.

Viktoria turns to us and smiles.

"She invites you to return to the child house in two days for his first birthday celebration. She says you're welcome to come regardless of the Judge's decision about this adoption."

She likes me! What a warm and kind gesture! Wait! We have to appear in court and soon! I thought a child protective review panel would handle this situation. Regardless of the judge's decision? What if he says no? What if Mikhail decides to interfere with the courtroom proceedings? I bet he knows the Judge. What if Mikhail influences the Judge?

I inhale a deep breath and wipe my tears away with my sweater sleeve.

Chapter 19

A quick check of the room validates my suspicion—the $200 dollars is gone, the penny replaced by a bullet.

"I think we should alter our appearance as much as possible," I tell Ethan. "Mikhail could be at the courtroom waiting with his men. It'll at least give us an opportunity to perhaps spot them before they see us."

"The way I see it—it couldn't hurt," Ethan says thoughtfully. "But if they are there to disrupt, it'll take place no matter how much we alter our appearance. Having said that, it'll give us a chance to buy some time to escape."

"All I need is some scissors so you can cut my hair. Will you look in the maid's closet outside the room?" I ask as I begin to strip off my make-up and apply dark black pencil under my bottom lashes, smearing it under my eyes to make bags.

After a few minutes, I hear fast feet outside our door, and Ethan returns breathless.

"Nothing in the maid's closet, but I saw a maid with scissors hanging on her cart. With a sweet pleading *pagalista* look, she let me have them," he says with a grin.

"Okay, start cutting—straight across the back. Make it shoulder length. Then, I'll cut your hair. You'll need to shave off your mustache too."

KELLY K. LAVENDER

"I think we need to find our darkest simplest looking clothes to lock-in the humble appearance we're aiming for."

After the scissors stop clicking and the hangers stop rattling, we look at ourselves in the mirror and see the Ellis Island immigrant version of ourselves, clad in dark simple clothing with a too-travelled look etched on our faces.

Gray skies and polar cold set the stage on our important court date.

Snowflakes pour from the sky like graffiti at a hero's homecoming. Only a few days after our arrival in Siberia, we'll be in court! Our enthusiasm ping pongs back and forth as we count the minutes until Natasha's arrival.

We share a cab with Viktoria and Natasha to the courthouse. As we open the door, Natasha's jaw drops.

"What did you do? You look not pretty! Your hair! It bad! And clothes! Do you lack good clothes?" She pivots in her seat to look back at us, grimacing at the sight.

"We needed a change to mark this special occasion. And we couldn't sleep last night; so, we're tired. We have good clothes. We merely want to look very serious today," Ethan explains smoothly.

"If I know you want hair cut and lack good clothes, I organize it, of course," she stews.

"We can do better than that!" she jeers, turning away brusquely. Ethan looks out the window to hide his growing smile while I look at the floor to hide my smirk. Natasha says little else, focusing straight ahead, her face twisted in disgust.

Ethan and I sit closer to one another and hold hands while ogling the scenery. Every so often, he squeezes my hand and we smile at one another, moony-eyed like newlyweds in the back of a limo leaving the church.

102

"Oh, I need to tell you something before we go into courtroom. I forget the American name that you choose for your son; so I select another name which will appear on all legal documents. The first name I remember—Zachary. I forget middle name."

"You what! Well, what is his name, Natasha?" I hiss.

I could just toss you from the cab, courtroom hearing or not.

Ethan squeezes my hand and smiles weakly, nodding his head in disbelief.

His expression says control yourself. We still need her. Yes, we do damn it! I never thought this adoption would also be a lesson in controlling fury.

"If you not like it, you can legally change it in the U.S," she says cavalierly, with a roll of her eyes.

I'd like to toss her out of the cab and run her over. Yea, Natasha, that's exactly what we want to do after dealing with a bureaucratic minefield to get here, go back home and change a name. Why didn't you just call to ask us the name?

The cab stops, and I look around to see a typical downtown setting for a mid-sized older city like Buffalo. People scramble multi-directionally like ants on an anthill. Aging one story and three story buildings dot the landscape. Parallel-parked cars line the streets. As we exit the car and cross the icy streets and sidewalks, I see a busy Baskin and Robbins ice cream shop. People scurry out with their ice cream cones back into the Antarctic climate.

I'd like to have a steamy hot chocolate from a warm, sweet-smelling Starbucks coffee shop. Speaking of chocolate, I'd like to take an ice cream cone and smash it into Natasha's face while she lay unconscious in the street. Then I'd pour my hot chocolate on her finery.

I smile; then, chuckle at the evil picture.

Natasha looks at me in frightened surprise.

She thinks she has me figured out. I shouldn't laugh now according to her calculations. I should probably laugh more often at her fuck-ups. It'd rob her of some of her gotcha power.

A slide and near fall re-directs my attention to the seriousness of the day. Hurriedly, we move into a plain, unofficial-looking building. After climbing a dimly lit flight of stairs, we huddle outside a closed door. Memories of work-related visits to U.S. courthouses race across my mind, "the beauty of bureaucracy" is apparently international. I scan the area for groups of machine gun toting men or police.

Good—no ponytails, no tattooed faces, no need for alarm yet. I need to find out how solid we are going into this courtroom. Maybe, I'll just chit chat with Natasha, the witch, to gauge her confidence level.

Once again, Natasha's wide eyes and rapid-fire diction tell the story. She acted this way the morning she arrived unannounced at the hotel room with those two women.

Nervously she glances around the room as if she's awaiting an attack. I remove my coat and the sweater under the coat and jokingly place the rolled sweater under my shirt to cover my B-cups.

"Would these breasts improve our chances of success?" I smirk.

Initially, Natasha stares at me blankly; then, a smile flashes across her face, and she roars with laughter. Grabbing an overcoat, she rolls it up and places it under her shirt and over her belly.

"No, I think that this, being pregnant, is most good for the courtroom," she cackles.

Our chorus of laughter fills the hallway, and for a brief moment, I feel normal—almost even in a good mood. Then, a door cracks open, and a clerk steps out, his face serious and drawn.

As he asks us to enter the courtroom, our laughter suddenly stops and levity vanishes.

For better or for worse, it's time to prevail or not.

Chapter 20

At this time, our group consists of five people—Viktoria, Natasha, Ethan and I and our court representative, Svetlana. As we walk the slowest of walks through the massive double doors, I review our last minute instructions:

1) Present the gifts to the judge and prosecuting attorney before the proceedings begin.

2) Remember only the translator may sit with you after court begins.

With sweaty hands, we present the expensive gifts, Dior perfume and Dior bath products, to all court officials. In the States, these gifts would be considered bribery.

With a nudge, Viktoria guides us to our seats in a narrow oblong room. By sitting three across so that Viktoria sits between us, we directly face the judge positioned on the short wall. We're sitting closer than I ever imagined we would be, sitting at the long wooden table in the uncomfortable wooden chairs. On the opposing longer wall of the room, the remaining members of our group face the prosecuting attorney. Of course, the prosecuting attorney, representing Dmitry, watches and waits in a position half the distance from our chairs to the judge.

We rise and state our names and ages to the judge. Viktoria then instructs us to sit as the judge reads the child's file aloud while she handles the translation, as usual.

"This baby is the result of a coupling between a student nurse and a doctor/instructor. The "father" refused to acknowledge the child citing "religious reasons". He attempted to persuade the mother to terminate the pregnancy. She refused. Angered by her refusal, he worked to have her dismissed from nursing school. With no means of support for the child, she had to place him in the child house."

What a brave Mom to stand up under that kind of pressure and do the right thing.

What religion would advocate turning your back on your child?

"'How close do you live to your families?'" The Judge begins.

"We live 30 miles away from both families," Ethan answers.

Leaning back in her chair, the Judge continues. "'How many people are in your family, Mrs. Evans? And yours Mr. Evans?'"

"There are three family members on Sophia's side that live nearby and three on my side," Ethan replies.

Leaning forward, the Judge addresses Viktoria rather than us.

"'How will you support the family, Mr. Evans?'"

"I work as salesman in the medical field. I sell medical equipment to doctors."

"'I see by your file that you've worked in this field for five years with success. That is good,'" the Judge observes.

Turning, she looks directly at me.

"'Will you leave your part-time job, Mrs. Evans?'"

Shit! I didn't know we'd be answering any questions.

"Yes, yes, of course, I will," I answer emphatically.

I want to compensate for his better than average, yet still unfortunate first year of life.

"'Why do you want a child?'" the judge asks.

Viktoria looks at me to answer first. My mind scrambles for a diplomatic response. We want to provide an extraordinary life for a child whose future seems crippled by a third world country which "parented" him—not diplomatic enough when spoken by the American. Given the career choices for a graduate of the broken adoption system, we want to positively change his life path with love and opportunity—not diplomatic enough either. Nervously, I look at the Judge and the clock above her head as time seems to stand still for me.

I'll use peripheral concepts—a love of children, a neighborhood teeming with kids and an ability to provide generously for him. We want to be parents and give him something the system can't promise— a loving nurturing home with a forever family.

As I begin to speak, my word and thoughts disappear. I can't condense all my thoughts and emotions into a single sentence.

"I…" A sob escapes my clenched mouth, my thoughts and words vanish, ground to ash. *What the hell is wrong with me! I'm crying the big waterfall cry. I need to talk and be articulate now. I've never done this before. I need to re-gain my composure. I'm so embarrassed.*

Who is this person?

***

I try desperately to compose myself, but I can't locate my "off button". The Judge says nothing. The room is quiet as everyone witnesses my meltdown.

Ethan looks at me in a soft, startled way. His puzzled look conveys more insight to the judge than any answer that I would provide. While I continue to cry, the translator turns to Ethan for a response.

Clearing his throat, he says, "We have a lot to offer a child. If we do become parents, it'll be the happiest day of our lives," he replies with complete sincerity.

Choking on my sobs again, I cough uncontrollably.

"'Hmm...'" The judge continues.

"'The next order of business is the waiver of the mandatory two week waiting period, should the adoption be approved.'" Viktoria translates.

"'I understand the baby needs surgery as soon as possible in the US.'"

Please don't make me affirm that statement. Circumcision is the planned surgery, not really a "need". Svetlana told us that wanting to expedite our trip home is not enough to warrant a waiver.

Stone-faced, I look at the Judge. Ethan grabs my hand as we await the next round of questions.

Viktoria turns to us, clasping her hand together. A never-seen-before smile plays on her lips.

"'The judge says that your adoption is approved, and you have permission to leave immediately with your son named Zackary,'" she announces as her eyes fill with tears.

"We did it! Zack is officially part of our family!" I announce as I fly into Ethan's arms.

Ethan and I hug each other with wild exuberance—a feeling only once shared before when we walked down the aisle on our wedding day.

As I look at Ethan, I see he's smiling while blinking back tears.

Natasha and Viktoria rush toward us for congratulatory hugs. Svetlana, who Natasha dubbed "the shark" after their private breakthrough meeting, coldly observes the scene.

I take a moment for a panoramic view of the room—looking for Ponytail or one of his team.

No Mafioso, no glint of guns in sight. Safe-for now.

Seeing an opportunity, Svetlana moves to my side. Roughly grabbing my arm, she whispers, "I never help you again if you go outside the system. You listen me. You never do this again. This make me worry of my life, my family. You work with Mikhail in this area next time. He police chief and has much power here."

I cringe at the thought of Mikhail and his thugs dealing with children, with Zack.

The scales of justice suddenly tilt heavily against us.

Chapter 21

Back at the hotel room, bittersweet success hangs in the air. Zack is our son now, but the threat of retribution dangles over our heads like a sword. Mikhail has a reason to join forces with Ponytail.

"What's our strategy now?" I mutter settling down onto the couch. "With Mikhail running the adoption business, we have two Mafioso who want to kill us."

"And a baby to protect," adds Ethan, raking a hand through his hair.

"Honestly, since Ponytail has support from Mikhail, we only have one option, the same option as before—keep our eyes open and stay alive until we reach US soil." Hours tick by as Ethan paces the room, periodically pulling the curtain aside to look out the window.

I'm staring at the page of a book, but my mind is elsewhere. When suddenly the phone rings, I jump up, toppling my book.

"Dad, I'm so glad you called! The Judge approved the adoption and the early departure! We're exhausted, but so enormously happy."

"I'm very excited for you. How soon can you leave?"

"In a couple of days."

"I want you to leave as soon as possible—no delays, no sightseeing."

He sounds stressed out. His voice is gravelly and tight.

"Of course, Dad, as soon as possible."

"What's wrong?' I ask afraid of the answer.

"It's Ethan's grandmother, Mimi. She's not doing well. The doctors are doing all that they can to keep her comfortable and alive until you return. I don't know if you want to tell Ethan."

"What's wrong with her? Have they stabilized her? How much longer does she have?"

"Old age and the move to the nursing home have taken a toll on her heart. After all, she lived in the same house for 50 years. She's stable now, but she's been on a roller coaster ride of ups and downs. The doctors aren't sure how long she has, it could be a month or a year if she's lucky. Meeting her grandson will make a huge improvement in her attitude."

My brain processes the information and adds it to our chaos:

Mimi is Ethan's favorite grandmother. She's kind, generous and loving. Since she went to the nursing home, she's been slow to adjust but healthy. No one thought she'd take a turn for the worse. He's right about Mimi meeting Zack, he'd be a huge boost to her life force.

I'll tell him tonight.

***

An hour passes, the phone rings again. Ethan grabs it before I can.

"You must come with me to dinner tonight at 7:00. We pick you up," Natasha demands.

"We're really tired. How about tomorrow night?" Ethan asks.

"No, it must be tonight. You have two hours until dinner. We meet people who helped with the adoption."

Ethan and I look at one another with weary eyes.

We'd just love to stay at the hotel to relax and reflect. This is not a time we want to eat dinner with people we don't know. We're emotionally exhausted. How can we say no? We're not out of here yet.

"Hey, honey, the phone call prior to Natasha's was from my Dad," I say as I look at the floor and then into his eyes.

"What did he have to say? "Ethan asks casually.

I walk over to him and hug him tightly.

"Well, Mimi is not doing very well. Her heart is faltering. She's been through a lot of changes lately with the move. She's stable now. Her doctor said she could live another month or another year. I'm sorry, Ethan."

He's suddenly still and quiet. I hope he can handle this extra baggage.

"Oh, that's bad. I knew she had issues with her heart. The big change in residence probably triggered all of that," he says.

Pulling away, he walks to the window staring out at the now unfolding blizzard conditions, strong tree-snapping wind and crippling cold.

"I know my grandmother—she'll pull through. She's tougher than all of us, but the sooner we go home the better. The thought of holding her great grandson probably is keeping her going," Ethan mutters. Turning, he looks at me. His eyes mist over with emotion.

"I love her so much and have so many good memories of her. Yea, we need to get out of this 'freezer'. Let's put this damn dinner behind us."

Willpower and discipline would have to carry us through the rest of the day. At 7 pm in the company of Natasha and Viktoria, we travel into the frigid Siberian night.

As we exit the hotel onto the street, I quickly scan the area.

Will Ponytail make his anger known now? Or at the restaurant? My gut tells me that he's watching and waiting—waiting for the moment to seek redemption for his humiliation at our hands.

The taxi stops in front of a small, one story building. As we walk through the dimly lit entry, I notice people huddled in every available space. We follow the smell of tantalizing food—spicy fish, baking bread and bubbling borscht. Pausing at the doorway of a private banquet room, we face fifteen complete strangers seated at a round table awaiting our arrival.

As soon as we sit, the doors to the room close. The wait staff hovers over the table to fill each shot glass and each water glass. As the waiter serves the last shot of vodka, a tall, dark-haired man stands up and taps his shot glass with a spoon. Looking at Viktoria, he apparently asks her to translate.

"Nikolai says-'We are here tonight to celebrate an adoption. With our help, Mr. and Mrs. Evans adopt a beautiful baby boy, Dmitry.'"

Cheers and the *clink* of shot glasses echo the importance of the occasion. A tsunami of vodka shots and toasts keep the celebration loud and raucous. The *clang* and *clatter* of silver serving trays being uncovered and forks and knives falling to the floor as the merriment escalates. Mirth served warm, occupies a spot next to the plates like a scoop of chocolaty decadence begging for another bite.

Remembering my father's warning about vodka, I begin to sip my shots as dinner progresses, hoping to survive with dignity. As dinner continues, introductions, conversations and toasts ricochet wildly around the room. Water glasses topple generating snickers and applause from the group.

Clearing his throat, Nikolai stands and again ceremoniously taps his glass. This time, Viktoria looks only at Nikolai as she translates.

"'For years, the US and Russia are enemies. Who can forget the Cold War? My brother and I are former soldiers. From time we were small, we were taught US is our biggest enemy.'"

From the corner of my eye, I see pickled Ethan sitting motionless as our host continues.

"Tonight, however, we embrace you as parents of one of our children. I hope that Dmitry will return here to find a bride and marry."

Return to Russia for romance! No way!! Zack's passport may be confiscated, and he'd be forced to serve in the military.

I cough as the vodka snakes its way down my throat.

If we return safely home, I'll never come back here.

***

Having said our good-byes, we hop into the van at 11 pm. As Ivan is about to close the back door, I see a short muscular man leaning on the outer wall of the restaurant. The outside light fixture clearly defines his silhouette. He contentedly smokes a cigarette. When he turns to look at us, his eyes lock-in. The smile on his face grows as he drags on his cigarette several times and spits on the concrete. After the van door closes, I smudge the window to see him again. I see everything I need to see. I see a ponytail and a knife attached to his boot.

Chapter 22

The dawn of a new day in Siberia marks a historic change in our lives. When I wake, I lie on my back staring at the ceiling, letting the truth sink in.

We are finally Zack's parents!

Ethan lies sleeping on his side turned away from me. I wrap my arms around his back and squeeze. He turns around to face me with his brightest smile. Then he kisses me on the forehead.

"I've never seen you this happy!"

"It's a big day! It's our first full day of parenthood—you know what that means?" I don't give him a chance to guess. "It means we get to go shopping for his first birthday party ever!" My red-hot glow would melt snow right now.

"Parenthood – yes! Shopping – er…okay," he says with mock glee.

"Let's eat lunch here and grab a taxi to go to the local mall," I say as I strip off my pajamas and start adding layers over my essentials—bra, socks and undies.

After Ethan preps for the cold, we go to the hotel restaurant for lunch.

"Borscht and sturgeon *Pozhaluysta,*" I tell the waitress.

I think that I'd really like to have red or black caviar, but this is easier to order. I've eaten this almost every day for lunch or dinner since I've been here. I wish I could interpret the menu.

Ethan orders the same, and we skip the carafe of vodka.

In the taxi, I sit next to Ethan, repeatedly craning my neck and using my small makeup mirror to look behind us and beside us.

Ethan cups my face with both hands and looks into my eyes with empathy.

"Come on, Sophia. You don't use your make-up mirror that much. Live in the moment! Be aware, but don't let him overshadow everything else. Let's *have* fun!"

He's right! I'll make the most of every moment!

Ethan leans toward me for a kiss. In an instant, I pull him forward on top of me and giggle as we kiss like sex-starved teenagers in the back of the cab.

The taxi slows to a stop and as we vault out, I gawk at the Pentagon-like "come hither" appeal of the beige building devoid of signs. As we climb several series of glazed steps, my eyes instinctively scan the area for beautiful products housed in carefully designed store windows, bold colors, appealing smells—any traces of retail seduction. Unfortunately, the retail orgy my eyes and pocketbook yearn for fails to appear as we walk into the only department store in the mall.

I sniff the air, stop in my tracks to make a 360 and look around.

This place reminds me of going-out-of-business inner city dollar store, a dollar store which happens to sell food, liquor, clothes, toys and holiday decorations. The beige mannequins on display so poorly represent clothing and products that I want to slap them for offending my sensibilities.

"From the look of the mannequins, you'd think hurricane winds blasted this space."

We both stare at the twisted-the-wrong-way wrists and arms of the mannequin used to model clothing. The mannequin is wearing a wool v necked navy top and pant and one navy pump. And she appears to be pointing at a trail of bras, underwear and socks that lay scattered on the floor. The other blue pump completes the scattered ensemble. Fallen pants and jackets drape over long silver hanging rods.

I close my eyes tightly and look away. It's as if someone struck me across the face.

This inhibits my shopping lust.

"Well, I didn't plan to shop for underwear and bras, but the heap on the floor is so appealing. Maybe, I should just pick up underwear and a bra off the floor and try them on." I snicker.

"Why yes you should. And the way her shirt is hanging off the shoulder, we may get a flash of her bulging breasts." Ethan grins.

Hopefully, the toy department will be better managed. Or so I hope.

As we walk to the toy department, I gasp.

"The toys are untouchable. You can't just grab them from the shelf and examine them."

"They're all lined up in a glass showcase," Ethan says in surprise.

"It looks like you have to line up at the counter and look."

"It looks like there is a crush of people at the counter to *look*," I observe trying to figure out the system. Scratching my head, I stand bewildered.

There is another line at the register, but no one is holding a toy.

"It looks like you have to stand in line to ask the register clerk to hold the toy. Watch. Then, she retrieves it from the glass case and stares while you examine it, "Ethan observes. *Good grief, she hovers over that plastic toy as if it's an expensive ring at a jewelry store*

"Then, you pay the clerk and go. Everyone waits in one line to hold, pay and go," he continues.

"It's amazing that people buy anything at all. You don't get to shop, enjoy the process and the choices. The urge to be the playful curious consumer prohibited. And who wants to wait in that slow-moving line?" I complain.

"We'll just make our decisions while waiting in this long line so we can get out of here."

"Okay, that's probably the best thing to do. I certainly won't doubt our choices or ask to look at different ones to make the best choice," I quip with gritted teeth.

This is so strange. We always find the best deal for the best price.

With smiles on our faces, we point out our choices, pay and leave the shopping fantasy gone amuck behind us. We purchase gifts for all of the children in the child house and a few clothing items for Zack. The "subway clean" staircase, there are no escalators, leads us down to the main floor for a final chance to purchase liquor and food.

***

Sitting in the cab, we enjoy our bounty—baby clothes and gifts, champagne, chocolates, cologne, small jewelry boxes and specialty soaps for the staff (as instructed).

What a wonderful experience! To be at this place, at this time, to buy gifts for all of the children and to celebrate our son's 1ˢᵗ birthday party with him before we leave.

"I'm just obese with joy today!" I exclaim as we exit the cab.

"My thoughts exactly," he says with a smile before grabbing my hand. "And the babbling brook united the cloud-covered city."

"You can mock me all you want! I'm so happy!" I answer, sticking out my tongue at him. He laughs and pulls me closer to him.

Nothing can ruin this for us.
Nothing.

Chapter 23

My eyes open suddenly and I stare at the ceiling in the dark room. It's 6:45 am according to the green glow of the clock on our bedside table. Ethan's snoring must have awakened me.

"Birthday Party! Birthday Party! It's time to wake-up!" I whisper, nudging Ethan frantically with my hand.

"Wake-up! Wake-up!" I nudge again with more urgency. "We need to get out of here!" "What's wrong? Is there a fire?" Ethan turns toward me, rubbing his eyes.

"No, silly. Today's Zack's birthday! Let's get started!"

"And ...It's 6:50 am. They aren't ready for us yet," he announces with a yawn.

"Can you really go back to sleep? Let's grab a quick breakfast and walk around or sightsee via taxi." I grab his hand as if to pull him out of bed.

"Okay. I'll call Natasha after breakfast and tell her we want to arrive early," he says, a feebly controlled smile playing on his lips.

Two taxis appear outside our hotel early this cold, sunny morning. For comfort, four people, Natasha, Viktoria, Ethan and I and our gift baggage and video camera, travel in two separate taxis.

"I wonder if we'll see the other children or just leave the gifts for them. I can't wait to see Zack's face as he examines his gifts." I smile, looking dreamily at Ethan. Leaning over, he kisses the tip of my nose.

"Whatever his reaction, we've got so much to be happy about," he says as he moves over to sit next to me. Grabbing my hand, he kisses it with courtly fervor.

"You're right. I'm so thrilled to be right here right now." Stretching up, I plant a kiss on his lips, giggling with joy.

As he puts his arm around me, I nuzzle into his chest as I stare blankly out the windows, peacefully lost in my thoughts.

For several miles, the taxis motors the waxy streets in caravan fashion as planned and discussed. Then, suddenly, our cab swerves left into an alley while the lead car maintains its course, heading straight down the road. The tires lose traction, and the back end slides.

I pull away from Ethan to look out of both windows.

Ethan taps the driver on the back, shakes his head (as in "no") and motions toward the lead car. The driver waives him away, instead checking his rear view mirror.

Good grief! What's this guy doing? The lead car is going a different way. How can he even drive that fast on these icy roads without flipping the car? You can't see black ice on the road.

Ethan and I stare at one another, wide-eyed.

He's got the same sinking feeling that I do.

Looking at my watch, I see twenty minutes pass as he screeches to a stop in the parking lot of an old decaying apartment complex. Without a word, he grabs the keys, jumps out and sprints to one of the units.

My thoughts race and spin.

"What's he doing? Why are we here? Do you think we'll be kidnapped or robbed? This is a third world country where money can buy anything. The Mafioso control everything here. Maybe, Ponytail is involved."

"I think we're in big trouble if he has some evil in mind for sure. He has the advantage."

"We can't just run since we can't speak the language, we don't know our hotel address or the address where we're going. We have no friends or family here. They don't even know where we are! We don't have Natasha's or Viktoria's phone number with us either!" My eyes dart nervously around the parking lot. Ethan stares blankly ahead, immersed in thought.

"Or maybe, the other cab will turn around and try to find us. They could be on their way now," I comment with counterfeit hope.

"I think we should look for an opportunity to run together— same time, same direction."

I look around for barriers of protection in the immediate area.

We should be at the child house with Zack celebrating his birthday now.

I bite my lip, tears beginning to blur my vision.

Gripping my door handle, I prepare to run. The driver returns quickly, jumps into the cab, without even a glance to the backseat, and speeds from the parking lot to unfamiliar streets.

No visible gun and no additional driver—definitely, a good thing.

Finally, we arrive at the child house parking lot.

Natasha and Viktoria stand outside waiting for us with arms crossed and frowns etched on their faces.

"What happened to you?" Viktoria glares at the driver as she speaks to us, her eyes flashing with anger.

Adrenalin, excitement, relief, and a Mimosa of a jolt, make me shaky as we stand on the sidewalk. I hold his hand to balance as he begins.

"The driver just changed course. It scared us a lot. He didn't or couldn't talk to us. We didn't know what was going on and we still don't," Ethan replies, his voice quivering.

Turning to the driver with a fiery expression, she lets loose a raging river of Russian fury. Natasha joins in, standing next to Viktoria, and yells, wagging her finger then jabbing it into his chest.

The cab driver appears shocked, dumbfounded at their reaction. And with that, Natasha slaps his hand with a wad of money, and shoos him away with a scowl.

Viktoria turns to us, her eyes wincing with wrath. She looks angry enough to ram her fist through a wall.

"He's an imbecile! He took you to his home because he forgot his cigarettes," she explains seething.

"Let's go see your child now," Natasha suggests.

A deep breath later we walk to the front door loaded down with gifts. We stand in the foyer inside the front door, waiting for someone to welcome us. I look left to see the child house manager smiling warmly at us. Motioning us into her office, she hugs all of us, offering congratulations.

Immediately, we present champagne, cake and gifts for the staff. As she looks down at her desk, the warm smile fades. Then, she carefully re-packs all items in the original traveling box, placing it under her desk.

That's unusual. Maybe, she thinks it's too disruptive to give those gifts now. Or did we trip over some invisible line of propriety?

As if on cue, after the manager hides the gifts, our son appears wearing a red holiday suit. Smiles brighten every face as the caregiver places him in my arms. Ardently, I cover Zack's head and hands with countless kisses while he rests comfortably and contentedly in my arms. My heart flutters as we share a warm embrace.

What a magnificent blessing to live in this moment! After all of this struggle, finally, he's here with us forever.

Euphoria saturates every cell in my body. I feel a need to check my sense of reality. I shake my head and blink intermittently as if to meld my mind and body together once again. Liquid jubilation sprinkles my baby's head and hands, removing all doubt. The manager says something to Viktoria.

"She said that they dressed him in red so that you can tell the difference between him and the other children. They call him American boy now," Viktoria says with a smile.

American boy. Suddenly, worry steals my cheer.

I bite my lower lip and gaze through the window at the winter storm that awaits us.

I hope we make it home alive.

Our bad judgment may make you Russian boy again.

Chapter 24

"Why don't we go upstairs?" suggests the manager. A nurse reaches for Zack before we begin our upward climb. The surroundings exceed my expectations. The yellow daisy speckled walls gaze at us, and the spotless floors mock my questioning eyes. In the center of a large square room, twelve happy children waddle and play within the confines of a large square play pen. Cribs placed end-to-end against the wall form the inner perimeter of the room. Some interesting toys stare longingly at the children from the display case near the entrance. I immediately observe an inactive baby lying on its back in a crib separated from the others.

"Why isn't this child with the others in the play pen?" I ask Viktoria.

"She is sick and must be isolated from the group," Viktoria answers.

A nurse plucks her from the crib, allowing me to hold her. She's stunningly beautiful, dark ringlets and Caribbean blue eyes contrast with her alabaster skin. I hug her gently.

I'd love to be your mother—to create a forever loving home for you. You're the only girl here I'm told. I know your forever family will find you, honey.

"The manager tells me that Russians keep their girls and will give up their boys first if necessary," Viktoria comments, her voice thick with remorse.

Viktoria looks very sad. None of these babies should be here. They all deserve loving families.

Noticing my obvious affection for this infant, the nurse pulls her from me while my husband nudges me toward the playpen to give gifts.

As each child smiles and squeals with happiness at his new prize, I feel deep gratification once again. One boy waddles immediately to Ethan as we lean over the playpen wall. He's completely adorable with his friendly, extroverted demeanor, big smile, dark hair and exuberant, joyful eyes. Excitedly, he unsteadily moves toward us with his arms outstretched to receive a hug and a one-way ticket out. I glance at Ethan in a curious way—the child "sees" only him and makes his way into his arms. With a funereal frown and watery eyes, Ethan grabs the little boy—hugging him longingly for several minutes. After lovingly placing him in the playpen, he pretends to turn away to locate another toy from our treasury. He wipes his eyes several times.

He's fighting back tears still. This baby boy is ...

I put my arm around his waist to comfort him knowing what he would say before he said it.

"He recognized me. He's the other boy we wanted to adopt. He's the one we couldn't get." He tells me in a tortured voice, looking down at the floor. Wiping his eyes again, he sniffles.

Why didn't they just let us adopt both boys? They could be brothers. My eyes burn with tears.

Of course, we asked and asked again to adopt both boys after Ethan met them in July, months earlier.

Oh, yea, Natasha said that officials denied our request because it would create a big uproar within the city and within the child house. They said many local people who worked inside the child house and inside the country wanted these babies. And since we mysteriously received top priority on the waiting list, we didn't want to push the issue and possibly jeopardize our future with Zack. Oh, yea, that was when Natasha called us greedy, arrogant Americans for asking and asking.

From the corner of my eye, I see the child house manager approach us with Viktoria.

"He'll be leaving with an American couple in two weeks," she explains to Viktoria refusing to meet our eyes, eyes filled with love, sincerity and compassion.

We smile and sigh like two tired hikers at the end of a stony slope.

I hope and pray that she's being truthful. In this situation, we question a lot. We'll never ever forget this baby boy. Zack will know him too, when he gets older and watches his baby videos.

The clamor of kids jostling for toys quickly changes the subject. Blonde haired blue-eyed twin boys gape at our toy treasury and us.

"A child house worker has adopted these boys," Viktoria communicates. Each boy receives an identical toy as we push forward to meet and greet each child.

In the scrambling throng of squealing kids, a blonde haired blue-eyed baby conspicuously doesn't rush forward, he lies on his belly next to the railing on the side farthest from the only door to the room. He screams loudly and kicks valiantly in his anchored-to-the-floor position. Although he's old enough to waddle, he doesn't. I study his eyes, squinting eyes that focus on the other kids.

"Why doesn't that baby join the group?"

"Down's syndrome," Viktoria says, her voice trailing off as she averts her eyes.

Oh, no! His future ....will be painful and sad in Russia. Like the American culture, Russians exalt physical and mental perfection—the weight, the teeth, the youth, the athleticism, the money and the success.

Instantly, I shudder at the thought.

Of course, most Americans want healthy, "normal" babies and the Russian citizenry aren't interested; so, at a certain age, he'll be transferred to a state-run mental hospital instead of the school for orphans, the separate school that insures the safety of the orphans by separating them from the "normal" kids in the general population.

As he screams and kicks wildly, I put a toy within his reach which he grabs; however, he continues to flail and scream. To comfort him, I lean over and place my hand on his back to stroke him. As I caress him and talk to him soothingly, his legs became still and the screaming stops. I continue to stroke his precious, little hands, and gently scratch his back. Now, this baby lies totally quiet and still.

How amazing is that! Touch and voice have such a big impact on him. This baby just wants to be acknowledged, talked to and adored. He wants to be ... loved.

My eyes fill with tears as I continue to talk to him while I touch his head and back.

A life-changing moment, a lesson taught by a toddler teacher about the transcendent power of touch.

I owe you, sweetheart. You just made me a better mother and a better human being.

As I leave his side, I notice the screaming and flailing begin again as if we never met.

"And here he is…" announces the translator as the nurse brings our one-year old baby boy into the room and places him in the play pen. Hurriedly, I rush to his side. With a big hug and a couple of kisses, I present him with a toy, which he carefully inspects.

Another little boy approaches us with a new toy in hand. Turning slightly away from Zack, I shower this little toddler with affection. Zack positions himself closer to me and shoves the little boy, seizing his toy.

Why in the world would he do that? Was it jealousy or the toy or both?

With toy tightly clutched in his hand like a trophy, he has my undivided attention and everyone else's, giggles waft our way as our playpen dictator parades his win.

As quickly and abruptly as the party begins, it ends—the manager motioning us toward the door. The baby with Down's continues to cry with the same unrelenting intensity as he did when I left his side—he never pauses, but coughs when he gasps for breath. A quick hand-off to Ethan and I move toward him to say "Good-bye.

"*Nyet!*" The manager says as she grabs my forearm.

Wrenching it away, I look her squarely in the eyes.

"*Da!* Today, the answer is yes—for him and for me. Tell her Viktoria. Please tell her."

Without hesitating, I walk over to him, lean over and tell him with loving caresses that he is magnificent, worthy of love and very special. Suddenly silent, I know that he knows; so, I leave.

Slowly, we descend the stairs engulfed by an incandescent plume of pure joy and smoky sorrow—we can't be a bigger family. The nurse instructs us to wait, and she will meet us in the office with Zack.

After placing Zack in my arms, the nurse tells Viktoria that we must remove all of his clothing because the clothes belong to the child house. No, he can't keep the clothes on his back to wear to his new home.

Luckily, prior to this visit, we received information about the exit process; so, we remove the state-issued red holiday outfit, the change of clothes clearly frightening him. The "alien" disposable diaper scares him even more. In the child house, children wear many layers of clothing for warmth and absorption; the staff checks and changes the children periodically. Cleaning clothes is far more economical than stockpiling expensive disposable diapers. Finally, we complete our task and say goodbye quickly. As we hurriedly and carefully position ourselves in the awaiting taxi, we steal a moment for a one-second kiss.

We can go home! We completed the final step—the child house.

As we ride along in the cab, I watch Zack lovingly. He stares at me with a furrowed brow, his lower lip contorted as he sucks inwardly on it. Not only does he look terrified, but his chest rattles loudly every time he breathes.

We must do something right away to make him comfortable for the 13-hour plane flight home. We need a doctor's help now to board that plane.

Chapter 25

"Feeding instructions–bottles of Kefir, the other supplementary substance, no lime juice, he doesn't like it, and no orange juice."

No lime juice! Why would you give a baby lime juice?

"Let's just keep him on the same meal plan until later. What do you think?" I look to Ethan for some comment as I stack the Gerber's on the kitchen counter.

"Sounds like a good plan especially with the long flight home," Ethan chimes in.

"Let's make a bottle for him now," I suggest with a smile.

Ethan, who loves to cook, begins to pull ingredients from the fridge and put them on the kitchen counter while I grab the bowls and spoons. He snatches one of something and watches it slowly writhe into the bowl, landing with a loud slapping noise. Then, he covers it with water and mashes the gelatinous white brick, which smells like sour milk, into a drinkable substance.

"Yummy, may I pour a cup for you, my dear?" He asks with a grin.

"Only if you share it with me, darling," I answer with a smile. "Shall I get two spoons? We can feed it to one another." Zack doesn't blink when offered the noxious bottle-hungrily finishing it in a matter of minutes

***

A big dinner, a busy day and loving arms which now rock him transform squirmy Zack to sleepy still Zack, his glazed eyes closing for longer and longer periods of time until he finally sighs and surrenders to sleep.

The first night spent with Zack—unforgettable. After dinner, we diaper and dress Zack in his footy pajamas. Ethan and I take turns holding him so that we can brush our teeth and change into our pajamas. Then, I crawl over the perimeter of stuff—baggage, shoes, everyday necessities, baby stuff, etc that we couldn't put anywhere else in this crowded apartment-and lay down on the left side using a pillow laid flat to create a buffer. Ethan, cradling Zack, lunges over the guardrail of stuff and places Zack in the center of the bed next to the pillow. Then, he lies on the other side—placing another pillow beside him to complete the pillow fence

"What do you think? Will this be safe enough for him?" I ask.

"We'll let him tell us," Ethan answers with a grin.

I don't think I'll sleep much anyway. I just want to watch him sleep. What a huge blessing and honor to mother this wonderful baby.

My eyes fill with tears as I think about our struggle and all the things we would do for him.

I'll do anything for him. I'll be the best mother he could ever want.

Zack's sudden wail startles me.

"He's not …comfortable," I determine.

I sit up instantly in bed, picking him up. And he stops. When I put him back in the buffer space, he cries again. After a few times, clearly, it's time to change the strategy.

"Let's just remove the pillow buffer so he can touch us while we're in bed. I'm too awake to sleep much anyway," I suggest to Ethan, whose bleary eyes beg for sleep.

"Okay, I'll try to get some sleep and take sleep watch tomorrow," he agrees with a smile.

Ethan endured a tough emotional day. Sleep watch, my pleasure.

I grab the pillows and position them toward the end of the bed underneath Zack. I glance over at Ethan on his back, feigning sleep an ear-to-ear grin giving him away.

Then, I lie on my back wide-awake, listening and waiting. The rustle of a blanket and the flutter of a touch on my lower arm, the miniature hand resting palm down on my arm.

Zack.

Did he ever get the security of sleeping in the same room with a protector? Or did he just listen to the cries of babies that fear the dark? Did the caregivers ever comfort the crying babies at night?

I beam and grab his little hand and kiss it, putting it back on my arm. That's when I notice his other arm stretched toward Ethan, the tiny hand placed on his upper arm.

Zack sleeps and cries intermittently throughout the night. When I comfort him, he returns to sleep on his back. He awkwardly extends his arms to maintain constant contact with each of us all night long—rooted to his Dad and Mom. A bond to weather the decades made tangible in a single night.

Does he realize in some way that we are his? Or does he yearn for that security and comfort in the dark that he never experienced?

As we begin the second day in the apartment, our first full day alone as a family, his signals become easier to decipher, the diapering process becomes highly efficient. Aside from the episodes of play and lavish affection, showers of hugs and kisses, we have to take the necessary steps to provide the American Embassy with documentation required for U.S. clearance. Fortunately, we easily schedule an appointment at an American clinic for a medical exam that same day. The three-minute medical exam and review of the paperwork give us much time to make more memories with Zack. Mid-day, as our baby naps in bed surrounded by pillows, Ethan and I sit at the kitchen table.

"It was like he velcroed himself to us all night long. It was amazing," Ethan reflects.

"It was so special to be there for him, to share that time with him. You missed out by playing possum. I'm on to you now. You can't play possum when we get home," I joke.

"Home…He's going to be the little prince at home," Ethan muses.

Abruptly, a strange noise interrupts our dialogue, killing all conversation. Like Mustangs in the wild listening for danger, we freeze and listen for the sound only to hear it again. While completely unsure of the "what" of the noise, we locate the "where" of the noise. Tip toeing toward the mystery sound, we end up near the bedroom where Zack sleeps. We move toward the bedroom only to hear it again. At this point, we stand mouths agape as Zack entertains us with his best "raspberry" noises, trumpeting to us like an elephant calling the herd. Picking him up, I "raspberry" back.

Ethan puts his arms around my waist, adding his version of the best "raspberry". It's time for a family hug with Zack at center point. Zack grips my arms tightly as if he's climbing a rope; then, he relaxes his hands and puts his head on my heart.

It feels so wonderful to laugh freely without a care.

After all, the worst is behind us now.

***

Our next step is to contact the US Embassy for an appointment later in the week. The translator needs two days to translate all Embassy-mandated paperwork for our appointment.

For the next two days, as instructed, we remain in the vault-safe apartment, left again to entertain ourselves. Zack continues to battle chest congestion—our US doctor suggesting by phone that we give him a recommended dose of children's cold medicine. With a 13-hour flight home, it's imperative that we make him comfortable, and everyone else on that flight. By chance, Natasha breezes through the kitchen during a quick visit. Immediately, she spots the bottle of American medicine, stopping in her tracks to scrutinize it. Carrying the bottle as if it was a dead rodent, she walks into the living room.

"You, Americans, overmedicate your children! I call a Russian doctor to the apartment for the boy. He put onions in his socks and wrap his chest with a mustard poultice to treat him," Natasha rages as her face becomes fiery red.

Mustard poultice would burn his skin! Can't let that doctor treat him. No way! How do you dance around that scenario without offending her?

Ethan and I lock eyes. He's as stumped as I am.

Dumfounded, we stare at her in disbelief.

We definitely need to find a way out of this. Yea, this will be a long problem-solving discussion.

Speechless, Natasha spins on her heels leaving in a huff slamming the door behind her.

"Can you believe that!" My eyes bulge toad-like out of face.

"Of course, the answer is no. We're not doing that."

"How not to offend and say no?" I ask rhetorically, tapping my finger on my chin.

"I know—let's tell her that our doctor said that we can't discontinue the medicine because the problem will get worse. He also told us not to do anything besides give the medicine," Ethan offers.

That's it!" I proclaim happily. "Good thinking. That's our strategy when we see her again."

***

"It's been two days since we've seen Natasha. What a relief!! Although, she could see that the medicine is working," I smirk.

"One more call to the doctor to report progress. It'd actually be good to have her here to make the international call. Guess, we'll have to wait a day," Ethan says with a sigh.

It's dinner time when someone knocks at the door.

Ethan answers the door, standing aside so Natasha can barrel in.

Without a greeting or acknowledgment, she rushes to Zack. Picking him up in her arms, she ignores his flailing hands and dour demeanor, looking into his eyes first then holding him close. That's risky—she can trigger screaming mode any second. I bet she's holding him close to listen to his breathing.

"He's better, isn't he?" I ask.

Turning her back to me, she returns him to his book on the floor. Ignoring my question, she glares at me before to turning to Ethan.

"Will you make this international call for us?"

"Of course."

While sitting on the couch, her eyes dart from Zack to the kitchen counter and back again before she hands the phone to Ethan.

"Dr. Black, he's improving. What now? Stay the course?" Ethan asks.

With a loud sigh, Natasha stands, smoothes her skirt and dusts her shoulders before standing to leave, another glare as she crosses the room acknowledges my presence.

As she exits, a smug smile takes shape on my lips.

It's sort of witchy, but it feels good to be right.

Chapter 26

The Siberian airport—a bustling, inviting environment broad brushed in steel gray and ready-to-crumble brown welcomes us. The unheated gate areas offer little square footage for standing or sitting. Warmly wrapped Zack doesn't cry, complain or care because I offer him an early dinner bottle and a toy. Both Ethan and I stare respectfully at the menacing, snowy climate through the ceiling to floor glass windows. While I shiver at the sight of the blizzard cold, a darting figure catches the corner of my eye. Just a blur of color, but it makes me pause. My eyes jump from face to face looking for something familiar or suspicious. The crowd is parting like zebras scattering for the onslaught of lions. I see a short muscular man barreling our way—a man with a ponytail. With each stride, the gun wedged under his belt peeks out from his brown overcoat.

What's going on? Who is that? Oh my God, can that be Ponytail? Here? Anna's words haunt me—"The police always find the best way to produce the result to hurt the most."

What do we do? I can't run with the baby! Natasha doesn't know to help us!

What will Ethan do now? Maybe, I have to change the subject.

In an instant, I hand Zack to Natasha and turn to face Ponytail—my face contorts in a hard tight mask, my teeth clench and my eyes fill with molten hate, ready to incinerate anything in my path. I stand tall and upright in fighting stance, my heart racing and my body quivering with rage.

You want to kill me? Fine, bring it on if my baby lives. Knees and elbows, knees and elbows are my only weapons now.

"What's happening here? Why is stranger running at us?" Natasha shrieks.

"Just take Zack. Ethan and I have to handle this. Not your problem," I say frantically as I train my sights on Ponytail, bolting my body down into the floor and plotting my offensive. I feel, but won't meet her penetrating gaze.

"He wants to kill us Natasha. Either Ethan or I should be able to escape," I add wistfully.

"Ethan, we've got to split and re-unite later in the airport." I grab his hand and squeeze it, keeping my focus on Ponytail.

Split... like my heart is splitting now as if halved by a meat cleaver.

I may not see Zack grow-up, but at least he will have his Dad. A hard lump fills my throat as tears well up in my now stinging eyes.

Ponytail approaches with a predator's pace like a too hungry lion closing in for the kill.

Natasha and Ethan are stepping sideways away from me, distancing themselves for the collision.

My blood channels ice cube cold, my chin tilts up in defiance as the back of his hand rips across my face, a stripe of blood painting the trajectory. The bastard's wedding ring probably cut me! I raise my forearm to shield my face as I step forward to become a spinning top of elbows and knees. I see him lift his machine gun to pummel my head; yet, it falls to the ground.

What the hell happened? Wide-eyed with surprise, I turn to see Ethan, rebalancing on his back leg. With a quick do or die jump, I escape Ponytail's reach. Looking at Ethan, I see his soft understanding eyes and a small smile before he turns to run.

"*Nyet! Pomoshch! On pytayetsya skhvatit' nashego rebenka!* He try to grab our baby!" Natasha yells as Ponytail scrambles to his feet in furious pursuit. People in the crowd are now staring, whispering and pointing. I see a large man with a black fur cap frowning and glaring his hands fisted at his side, an enraged rhino not more formidable or fierce.

Ethan stepped up to protect us! I love you more than ever, Ethan! Find your way back to us! Maybe, someone will block Ponytail to give Ethan a chance to escape.

Natasha nudges my arm just as Fur Cap spins around in Ponytail's direction. Fur Cap heaves his big frame forward and runs fisting his hands—rhythmic and powerful like pistons in a car engine.

"I know what you are thinking, but you must stay here. You cannot help him now. Let's get on this plane and get out of here. I want to hear everything about angry man," Natasha says glowering.

Taking the baby from her, I hold him tight as the onlookers begin jockeying for a spot in line, the re-formed crowd of passengers becoming a turbulent waterfall of bodies rushing toward the resentful outdoor holding pool to board the plane. No one seems to care that I'm holding a baby as they shove us around to get closer to the front of the line. Natasha becomes angry and uses her body to create a comfort zone for us like an offensive lineman protecting the running back.

As I step forward cradling Zack, I realize that slippery ice thickly covers the runway. Holding him tightly to my body, I quickly check his protective armor of clothing. The merciless cold frisks us quickly with heartless fingers, searching for signs of vulnerability. With small respectful steps, I travel to the staircase.

As I look down at him, my foot skates out from underneath me, forcing a struggle for balance. My torn anterior cruciate ligament strains and bends, multi–directionally like a ribbon of cardboard attached to a large barbell, as I try to recover. Grabbing a fistful of Natasha's coat, I steady myself.

Must not fall—not with Zack. I can't drop him or fall on him! Natasha should be carrying him, not me! She's comfortable with this ice because she grew-up with it.

"Please, carry him to keep him safe," I ask as I stare at the icy staircase.

"Yes, of course." She smiles as she pulls scowling Zack from my arms.

With a deep sigh of relief, I look down at the ice and back toward the plane.

Great! The old weathered Aeroflot plane looks like it's ready for the scrapheap or a museum. I hate putting our baby on this plane. A vintage plane to battle the ferocious arctic weather as we travel to frigid Moscow. I may drink a shot on the plane this time too. Maybe, the leaks and the creaking cabin won't be exponentially irritating.

After we settle into our seats, Natasha turns to me with a commanding stare and an accusatory finger.

Will Ethan be able to escape and board the plane? How will we find him? Did Ponytail catch him? What will he do with him?

"We have a lot to discuss, but first hear me! Be invisible and careful with your baby—especially if he cries—every woman and stewardess watch you deal with him on plane."

"Now, tell me why that man wants to kill you and Ethan," she asks, her voice crackling with burning embers, which glow in her gaze.

***

Without a single temper tantrum, we reach our Moscow destination with extra baggage, two large carry-ons of physical exhaustion and emotional fatigue.

Finally, our son moves closer to home. We're much closer to our destination, but Ethan could be dead or enduring torture. Burning tears spill onto my face, patted and smeared away by our curious laughing baby.

For Zack, the traveling experience is sensory overload—unrecognizable sights, new smells, new people and a new place—total submersion into the world of the unfamiliar. His wide eyes dart around restlessly as he snuggles into me.

Before disembarking from the plane, I once again ask Natasha, the seasoned soldier, to carry him. And, still, each slow, methodical step forward on the wax paper-covered metal steps scares me. To add an extra measure of assurance, Viktoria follows as back perimeter coverage.

Well if I fall, I'll try to make sure it's backward and not forward, onto Natasha and Zack. With that thought, I pause to put more distance between us.

After we enter the brown and gray airport terminal, we spot Ivan who greets all of us warmly; then, he guides us outdoors to the white lacquered van. Working feverishly as if to beat a stopwatch in a racecar pit, Ivan assists us into the van and starts it before returning to the terminal to locate our luggage. As he drives, ice continues to paint and lacquer the inner and outer glass on the van windows reducing the entire 45 minute journey to the apartment to streaks of color. The car heater never overpowers the December cold inside or outside the vehicle, especially, this winter, the coldest winter in a decade. Zack sleeps with a wrinkled brow and active pacifier, safe and comfortable.

Safe and secure—my hope for Ethan.

A quick turn reminds me that my seat belt is unfastened. Without baby car seats, that was the only safety option to protect us.

"Where are the seat belts?" I ask while groping around the seat crevices with one hand.

"Russia cars aren't equipped with seat belts," Viktoria replies with a patronizing smile.

Good Grief!!! I bet air bags aren't standard issue either. I'll bet that accidents are more severe than they should be, no baby seats, no seat belts and no airbags.

"What happens after a car accident here, Viktoria?"

"When no serious injuries are involved, the situation is settled immediately with dual pay-offs to the law enforcement officer and the victim. We don't have lawsuit abuse here," Victoria proclaims, a proud smile pasted on her lips.

Finally, the van stops at the apartment. Thankfully, Ivan gently takes Zack from my arms and nonchalantly walks the opaque sidewalk surrounded by Christmas card snow.

I'm so glad Ivan is carrying him for me. You could carve bifocal lenses from the ice on that sidewalk.

With all of the stealth of a great grandmother, I approach and struggle with the short flight of outside stairs leading to the entrance of the apartment building. Ivan, Natasha and Viktoria wait patiently at the entrance while I complete the short distance. Ivan opens and closes the front door behind us and the temperature suddenly warms as the building blocks the cold wind.

Apparently, all we need is a light bulb for heat and light to climb the stairs to the second floor. I'll carry the baby and Ivan will take the bags. It's surprising. There are no elevators even in this luxury apartment building.

Finally, the last of the series of triple secured doors unlock and we part company with the group. Now, I've got to learn and understand Zack's signals. And more pressing—diapering. I lie Zack on the bed in his thick mummifying one piece jumpsuit. His arms and legs can't flex and move; so he lies on the bed like a scarecrow in ski wear. While changing his clothing to make him more comfortable in the warm apartment, I notice his tightly clenched fist.

"What do you have Zack?" I ask as I pick him up, hug him and scratch his little back.

"Can Mommy see?" I kiss his downy head and the top of his little fisted hand. He relaxes his grip to show me his favorite little toy from the child house—a simple thin white plastic dog with a round red belly (a ball attached on two sides so that it could be rolled with the touch of a finger).

Oh, my! His favorite toy from the child house! How did he do that? Did a staff member give it to him? He was a favorite baby in the child house maybe...

A passing thought about how Ethan would've roared with laughter about this discovery interrupts my emerging smile.

Tonight, it's toys, play, diapers and food for us, Zack. We bond as a family tonight, but tomorrow, we concentrate on making our family whole.

Grabbing one of Ethan's shirts, I place the long sleeve on the pillow boundary. Carefully cradling Zack in my arms, I lay him in his pillow "crib"—placing the shirtsleeve in his small curious hand. Watching his eyes widen in sudden wonder, I smile away the threatening tears. After tucking the other sleeve under the top mattress, I kiss him gently on the head and grab another of Ethan's shirts to layer over my pajama top. Pausing, I slip it on—wrapping myself in his woodsy orange aroma. Climbing in on the other side of the bed beside the pillow crib, I take Zack's hand for another kiss and move my arm into his outstretched fingers, waiting for him to become still.

Chapter 27

With the how-to-call-me-from Russia slip of paper in one hand, I push the buttons on the apartment phone with the other to phone Dad.

The big hairy coconuts emerge again to remind me how I hate to tell my Dad that I've made a mistake, that we've made a mistake. Get it right the first time, always his motto. Yea, one big hairy coconut wedges in my throat, its rough exterior scratching my throat making me choke and cough, and the other lies on my stomach like a bad meal. This happens every time I've been in this situation with Dad.

"Dad, Ethan didn't board the plane with us. I don't know where he is. I only know someone chased him in the airport, someone who we scuffled with in the hotel bar."

"What! I surround you with people to protect and guide you. And you still get into trouble! What's this about a bar? Why were you in a bar? I told you nothing good ever happens in a bar! Natasha is so careful… Wait a minute! She wasn't with you. Was she?"

"No, she wasn't, Dad," I mutter, shifting my weight from one foot to the other as I stare at the floor.

"What an idiotic thing to do! That was dumb, dumb, dumb! You said 'we scuffled.' I don't even want to hear the details. You were asking for trouble just being there. All this work and effort at risk because you two had to go to a bar! Maybe, you all are too immature to be parents! It may have been an awful decision for me to help you in the first place! The baby…is the baby ok?"

I know his face burns scarlet red, and his head shakes back and forth in vehement denial of the entire situation as if physically denying it would erase the reality.

"He's with me, Dad—doing well. The scuffle happened before we took custody. We have no good explanation for going to that bar. It was a lapse in judgment. It was stupid! Can we please skip the details and figure out how to find Ethan?" I plead weary from the assault. While I rub my forehead and stare at the floor, a migraine threatens to bubble up under my messaging fingers.

Dad doesn't need to know all the details—the assault and the wounded assailant.

It's over. The focus has to be on finding Ethan now.

"Haven't I done enough? What do you want from me now?" he asks acidly.

"You have, Dad, many times over. And I'm so eternally grateful. Can we find Ethan? And create a strategy from there?"

"Of course, but we haven't finished this conversation yet," he adds.

"Obviously, Natasha knows since she was at the airport with you. Maybe, she knows some people who can give us answers. What a mess! I'm so disappointed in the both of you!" He rants, leveling my hopes of even a short reprieve. I can almost see his blazing green eyes reducing my plan to a pile of ash. He continues.

"Honestly, Natasha did what I asked—her work is complete. They are under no obligation to do anything more now. I'm not going to ask them to appear on the radar screen, to risk their hides to help your out-of-control husband get out of jail. You've got a big problem on your hands. The truth is if this is too complicated and too long-lasting, you'll have to consider raising Zack by yourself."

***

The wooden rectangular clock on the tv shows two o' clock, and Natasha will be here any minute. After my conversation with Dad, she calls insisting that we meet at the apartment. A rustle at the door followed by a quick knock announces her arrival.

Snowflakes cover her fur hat and coat. Stomping the brown "gelatin" off her boots, she looks at me warily like a suspicious parent waiting to hear the next lie.

I haven't been outside. I haven't tried to call the local police.

"I found him, Sophia. He's in jail, charged with resisting arrest, rape and human trafficking."

I stop breathing as I process the information—sorrow watering my eyes. Grief finds my frown and elongates my face. My shoulders and knees burn with the burden of desperate can't-see-the-light sadness. Shrugging my shoulders and shaking my head, I begin to ask the follow-up question.

"*Da,* they know about baby," Natasha adds as if quoting a statistic from a business report.

They are charging him and holding him on crimes THEY committed at the bar! Are you kidding me?

"Did you see him? Is he okay?" I ask, as bitter dread pools in my throat.

"I saw him. He is okay. He is not dead. He has two black eyes, broken lip and crooked nose. His arm is … in a tie around his neck and he walk slow and strange. He wants me to tell you that he loves you, and he find a way to see you and baby."

What the fuck! Wasn't it enough to win by capturing him? Those bastards!

"Is this normal procedure for police here? "

"*Da,* of course, if a person do not follow rules. They poison people for not follow the rules," Natasha comments casually as if we're talking about a jay walking offense.

"He didn't break any rules or laws!"

"There are… how you say? Not written rules that our citizens follow—like being nice to authorities. Just like in your country."

Well, she's right—this could happen in a small town, but several people would have to lie for the charges to stick. And I doubt poisoning is possible. What does that matter though now! I don't care! We just have to free him!

"All the witnesses at the bar. Will they lie for the police? Because they fear the police?" I ask already knowing the answer, but struggle to uncover a diamond of hope.

"Of course, they will. They don't want to be hurt. They know the rules."

What now? Obviously, we have to get him out, but how? The group from the bar "own" that jail. Will she and her associates bail on us as promised if something goes wrong?

"You know Mafia always find the best way to hurt a citizen," Natasha murmurs as if she's reciting an elementary school pledge.

And they hit the bull's eye!

I thought there may be trouble at court when we were so close.

They knew about Zack, and they waited. They waited until we were together as a family and close to the plane, the plane to Moscow. Moscow is the place where we could easily be "lost" to them.

I unclench my jaw and relax my gritting teeth to form a new question.

I have to step out of "hissing cobra"mode to relax my body and think.

Quickly, I look around to look at sleeping Zack bordered by a fence of pillows. His binky bobs in his busy mouth, his lashes flutter and his little hands are balled-up fists.

A smile takes hold—immediately transforming for me.

I swallow the walnut in my throat and ask, "So, are you going to help us?"

Chapter 28

"Help! I help you now, and I don't like you! I only do because my boss wants me to. My work complete! I already do more than I must. I asked friends to find your husband. Look where we stand, you stay here in luxury apartment in Moscow! You given too much already! And you want more?"

"Thank you," I say, "but is there anything else you can do for Zack, for us?"

"What now! Do I break jail doors? You both stupid to go to that bar! I told you that you must stay inside since you arrived!" Natasha fumes.

"Look, I just need information, information to form a plan to free him. You're right—you've completed your assignment. You're right—we were stupid and reckless! If I could change this now, I would, but I can't. I have to move forward. And Natasha, thank you… Thank you again for what you've done."

My shoulders slump as I stand in front of her, my eyes searching the floor.

"That's hard for you to say," she cackles, her eyes becoming brown slivers. She takes a step closer to me, putting her hands on either side of her waist.

"You should say it months ago! You think it was easy? I never do this before! You and your husband are not enough good for Dmitry! Dmitry should stay in Russia with Russian parents!"

"What do you want from me? What do you want me to say? We've thanked you multiple times. What more can we do? Should we give up Zack because you don't think we're worthy of him?" I meet her stare with frosty acknowledgment, my eyebrows arching. Crossing my arms over my chest, I wait.

"I'll ask Sergei what he wants me to do! I have enough of you this day!" With an abrupt spin, Natasha storms toward the door, slamming it as she exits.

I don't know if she'll help. I don't know how long I can stomach her without trying to strangle her. It takes every drop of dignity and strength to ask for her help, but I'll do it for Ethan and for Zack.

***

Three days pass since we talked. Zack entertains himself at times by watching tv and playing with his toys. When he and I play, I can't think about Ethan—how's he being treated, how bad his injuries are and how he must be feeling. It haunts me except when I'm playing games with Zack or feeding Zack. Nights are the worst when Zack is asleep. I want to see Ethan, comfort him and help him, but of course, I can't because it's too risky. Zack could lose me too. Every night, it's just me against my demons—the what ifs, the how tos, the worst case.

While sitting at the kitchen table drinking a cup of tea, the phone rings.

"The good news—Sergei is your hero. He tell me that I must help you to have Ethan and be...How do you say? Invisible. He tell me two days ago when I asked him. I call friends in Novosibirsk and ask them to visit Ethan again."

Ok, what did I expect? She knew days ago that she had to help me and didn't tell me. I won't be angry. It's the least of my worries now. The important things are help and eyes on Ethan.

"How's he doing now?" I ask, worry carving into my moment of joy.

"Bad news—his arm is more bad, dirty with green and yellow. He ask for doctor, but no one cares. No doctor sees him. He is nervous now. He hears them talk about him many times in the day. He say to tell you not to worry that he has hope still."

His arm is infected! Fuck! Can you imagine the roaches and rats in that place? They won't call a doctor for him because they don't care if he loses his arm!

"What can be done? Can we send a doctor to see him in jail?"

"Nothing can be done now. Prison have doctors. No reason for another one. What can I say?"

"They enjoy see bad prisoners suffer, and they see him suffer, "she explains coolly.

Sounds like more government speak, middle school mantra.

"But he can lose his arm to gangrene! You know that! "I say.

"That is most small of worries now." Natasha says, shrugging her shoulders.

"Losing his arm is a small worry? What does that mean?" I gulp a shallow breath, casting my eyes at the floor, afraid to hear what she'll say.

She lowers her voice. "They send him to Vladmir Central soon. It is the prison for the most bad prisoners."

Chapter 29

The morning sun warms the apartment and marks the beginning of a new day and another night of fitful slumber. I watch Zack wiggle and grab fistfuls of air as he sleeps. Rising, I wash my face and dress for the day. With a cup of tea in hand, I sit and stare at the clock, it's 7 am, and I count the minutes until I can talk to Natasha.

"Will you come over and help me understand this?" I beg.

Natasha sits with me at the kitchen table. We're not speaking while stirring our cups of tea, our thoughts turning over in unison. The clanging of the spoons against the cups reminds me now of a bell chiming the passing of time, critical time—time that medically deprived Ethan suffers in jail and soon-to-be prison.

"Thank you for coming, I say, trying to keep my voice steady. I'm not angry with you, but I have to ask you. How is any of this possible? There's been no trial." My worst fears hammer at my now throbbing head as Natasha's words slash my heart to a bloody pulp.

Natasha's eyes look away from my glazed stare. Clasping her hands together in front of her stomach, her nose twitches in disgust as if she'd bit into a rotten apple.

"What? Please tell me." I ask, forcing myself to remain calm. My brain begins to blast answers.

There was no trial, but how would we have known about it if there was? They don't want him to be represented. It's easier that way.

I listen and watch as if Natasha is wielding a weapon, pointed at me.

"Wait! Did you know that this would happen? Did you think this would happen? Why isn't it enough for him to do some jail time?" I glare—standing now, hands on my hips.

"I knew a chance of it. Nothing to do to stop it. No jail time. He too angry about what happened when his friends watch," she answers looking out the window, talking to the window.

"Not sure about trial. No difference. Judges and the Mafia make it happen," she remarks blinking her eyes.

"When does he go? Where is he going?" I ask, my voice quivering.

"They don't say when. Vladmir Central is far away, 700 miles from Moscow. I ask about it. Stalin's son went there and Cold War prisoners. It is old and most feared prisons. It take people who make worst crimes. Not all prisons do. The guards carry Siaga AK-47s on backs. And prison dogs, big mean dogs that stand up at 6 feet and weigh as much as 200 pounds. Dogs can stop like 45 gun. Viktoria tell me all about it. Dogs are call Caucasian Mountain Shepherds. She tell me people angry about Vladmir Central. People say unfair treatment and inmate abuse. All I know now."

My mind stumbles, tripped by negative nagging emotions. I step backwards to distance myself from the tsunami of worry. Shaking my head in denial, I clear my head to think

Things just went from horrible to worse. Tuberculosis is rampant in those prisons, and he'll have a roommate, a roommate who may be a fighter or a murderer. And his arm is infected. And he is non-confrontational, and he says inappropriate things unintentionally. And he could die in there or be killed. Maybe, he'll find a way to be thrown into solitary, but that would require a fight with a bad arm or having contraband. He needs money to buy shanks or knifes. He probably doesn't have any money. He'd risk being beaten-up by the guards or attacked by the dogs if he chooses solitary. And I have to stop this train of thought now. It can make me crazy.

"Can we stop this before he goes there? What can we do?"

"Can I see him?"

"The most bad thought! You stupid girl!" Natasha barks at me. Leaning forward, she tilts her nose up and glares at me. Her eyes are like those of an angry cobra, unwavering and hard.

Ignoring her stare, I continue.

"I can dye my hair again and cut it shorter. Binding my breasts would be easy with sticky tape. All I need is loose clothing."

"It can be done, but it stupid," she says, pausing to glance at Zack.

Don't say it. I'm a mother now, of course. I can't put myself at risk because of him. I've got to think differently now. Zack can't lose both of us.

"Like I say you don't deserve him! You are not rich! He will not have brother and sister to play with like my son! I hate to be in this!" Natasha yells.

She's right, but she's wrong. We do deserve him. Maybe, the visitor can get a picture of him. Dealing with Natasha is—once again a nightmare in itself, but I have no choice.

Drumming my fingers on the table, I avoid her stare—waiting for the tempest to fade. Daring a glance when I hear her breathing become more rhythmic and deeper, I see her staring down at her cup of tea as if some answer would float to the top like a life jacket in a pool.

"You're right I'm just thinking out loud," I comment in my library voice, half-talking to myself and half-talking to her.

"What is thinking out loud?" She asks with a raised eyebrow, her eyes suddenly sparkling with curiosity.

"Just talking ideas before analyzing them," I answer matter-of-factly before sipping my tea. Watching her sip her tea, I see it. It registers like a flare. My mind zeros-in to study every nuance.

The sour scowl, the black marble eyes, the fisted hand—the volcano is about to erupt again. She has something to scream about again and she can't resist. Maybe, if she gets it all out of system, maybe she'll drain her fury like a doctor drains a boil. Then, it's over. And we can talk about my picture.

"You are good at that! That why we are here! But your talking ideas are stupid! You have no smart!

Okay, to an extent, she's right. How do I placate her? Need a different approach.

"You know I agree with you. You can teach us a lot." My eyes follow the once again stirring spoon in my teacup.

Slowly gazing at her, I see her mouth twist in a half smile. She avoids my eyes as she stirs her tea.

"I go now. Enough of you for today." She mutters calmly as she rises, raising her teacup for another sip. Pausing at the sink, she places her teacup in the sink and turns toward the plastic grey trashcan sandwiched between the sink and the fridge.

What is she doing exactly?

Leaning over and grabbing it with both hands, she pulls it easily from its berth and hurls it like a discus thrower.

Is she throwing that at me? The gloves are off, girl. This is a whole new level of fighting. I may not be able to control my need for retaliation.

I feel the fire building in my heart. The taste of iron blankets my tongue.

"This trash is you! No brain, no good! All bad!" She laughs as tea bags, dirty diapers and soup cans spill onto the floor like a cascade of garbage released by the trash collection truck. A ball of a dirty diaper rolls across the floor and collides with the table leg, exposing a messy stinky goo. A soup can *clinks* across the floor drizzling a stream of its red contents along a path to the other table leg.

"You know that really isn't a good idea," I say as I walk menacingly toward her. My hand hooks a chair sending it crashing to the floor.

"I'm much better at fighting than I am at restraint, that's what the bar taught me."

"Do you want to do this?" I stare straight through her, flames of anger licking my skin and melting away all reason.

Chapter 30

A torch flares, it's me, me hating, me plotting. "Two can play this game? Are you ready for that?" I hiss.

With my eyes trained on Natasha, I cautiously grab and re-roll the exposed diaper. I toss it up in the air like a baseball and catch it. With a knowing smile, I look at her with dancing eyes, glittering as if showcased by ballroom lighting.

"Used properly, this can be a tool—a weapon even. I've prevailed in the worst of circumstances, and I'm feeling really good about this particular fight." Ice coats my words with a chilling certainty that my unfeeling alligator glare reinforces.

I now know what it feels like to be a successful alpha predator, an uncaring dangerous creature invited to fight. I like it. Now, it's not because I can weather it, but because I can win it!

Unfolding the diaper carefully and cupping the clean backside, I look up at her with an unflinching stare. A small arrogant smile roosts on my lips.

"Not now, maybe later," Natasha says as she waves her hand at me in a go away motion. Turning to stare at the TV, she speaks to me.

"I was once young and stupid like you. You have to think about things above yourself now like how to stop Ethan move to Vlad Central. What do you choose to do with your energy anyway?"

Of course, she's right. I'm robbing Ethan of time that should be spent concentrating on him.

Avoiding her gaze, I roll-up the diaper. My shoulders drop, my eyes revert to normal mode and a surge of cool calm fills me like the refreshing breeze of comfort on a scorching hot day.

"Of course, can we find out when he will be transferred? "

"Anything more?" Her eyes search mine for more words.

She didn't apologize so neither am I. We just need to let it lie.

"I'll contact the US Embassy in Moscow and let them know what's happened. Maybe, they have some ideas."

"Maybe, we can hire a doctor to see him and treat him," I suggest looking at her strangely soft eyes.

"I'll try to do that and get a picture," she smiles.

Weird! Why is she acting so weird! So agreeable? So accommodating?

"Why don't we hug and make peace before I leave?" She suggests matter-of-factly.

Well, that might be a good idea. Her way of apologizing and mine too, without a lot of drama. Okay.

I look at her fidget as I walk toward her, her hand fisting in an open and close motion. Her lips twitch slightly, and her eyebrows rise as I draw near.

What's this? Should I be nervous about her or is she nervous about me?

My skin is crawling.

Maybe, I shouldn't do this.

Pausing, I study her look and body language.

My shoulders and neck suddenly feel polar cold. Chill bumps arise like a rash on my skin.

My low cut shirt is probably not warm enough for this apartment, but that's not it.

"What do you wait for? I must go," she exclaims as she covers the distance between us.

Grabbing me in a bear hug, she squeezes me hard, leaning back, lifting my feet off the floor. Releasing me, she shoves me against the wall and presses her forearm into my throat. Her smile grows as she leans onto her arm, her eyes glittering with joy.

I can't believe this is happening! Is she trying to dominate me or make me faint? Detach and think! Can I stomp her instep?

I squirm to put myself in position.

"Ivan show me yesterday for defense. Is good. Yes?"

"You be a good girl or I take away your air. Momma can't be a good momma with no air."

She whispers her nose almost touching mine, the scent of black licorice and roses burns its way up my nostrils, a stunning punch to my olfactory system. Dark circles frame her eyes and strands of hair surrounding her face are matted. There is a streak of crusty dried blood near her hairline at the cheekbone.

Zack screams loudly from the next room.

He's awake! Scream, baby. Never been glad to hear that until now. It's a distraction. Surely, she'll let me go! Don't move! Just wait.

With a smile of satisfaction, she gazes down at me like a conqueror on the battlefield.

Hoarsely she says, "Now, it is time to be Mommy. From bitch you change to Mommy. You be surprised how you can do it. I was."

I raise my free hand and slap her, my hand cracking like a whip across her face.

With a hard quick shove, she sends me to the floor, bursting into laughter.

"Young , stupid and full of fire. I like that, I love that. It makes it good for me." She announces, heading for the door.

Just outside the door entryway, she turns, looking over her shoulder.

"Don't forget to lock the door, darling."

Chapter 31

Rushing to Zack's side, I hold him close, kissing the top of his downy head. His tiny hand squeezes my arm as he follows my eyes.

I cross the room to the kitchen, grab a bottle and warm it. Sitting down in a chair in front of the TV, I cradle Zack in my lap. I offer him the bottle and stare at the TV not caring that ZZ Top appears on the screen.

A reminder of home, it's so remote now. You'd think the United States disappeared altogether. There's no news about the US, not even anti-American propaganda. It's like it vanished from the world stage.

With a sigh, my mind swirls, a vortex of competing problems, a tornado of refuse threatening to destroy my family. My thoughts travel home.

I should feel safe here at ease like at the farm, sitting in the sunshine using my bare toes to rock back and forth on the porch swing. Calm, safe and still like the pick-up truck sunbathing in the driveway, waiting for the next request. Ethan would be napping inside, the birds chirping and the leaves rustling outside. But in a breath, the weather can shift, and the black spout marches across the horizon, grabbing and tearing a path to us. It hurls cows, cars and trees in all directions, widening its swath of destruction, a sharp saber of sudden change. In the dark of night, it's the worst as we lie in bed next to one another unaware that it's coming.

Suddenly, no spoken word is audible, and the raging fury of the storm—a production of lightning, crashing sounds and breaking glass—is visible from our bed, the French doors framing every moment like a big screen TV. It feels that same way now like we're in the eye of the unforeseen undoing of our lives.

Zack leans on me sound asleep, his weight like a 10-pound sack of potatoes slung over my shoulder. Carefully, I place him on the bed using the pillows to fence him in.

Slipping in next to him and resting my head on the headboard, I reflect.

What will I do the next time she stops by? How do I stop this? I need her. She has the connections and the knowledge to help Ethan. Maybe, the Embassy will help us to help him.

I can't tell my Dad. If she's fired, it'd cause a delay to find someone else, someone else who can find Ethan and help him. And if she's vindictive, she could wreck any attempt to rescue him and keep Zack safe in Russia.

Yes, I'll call the Embassy in the morning and tell them everything.

***

My eyes blink several times as I wake up. Panicked, I look over at Zack. I'm sweating and my heart beats loudly—the rhythm of someone angrily using an axe to fell a tree. My mind scrambles to rake my swirling thoughts into a neat pile.

What caused this? The Embassy...must call the Embassy. And...Natasha's demeanor.

Must call the Embassy...but I can't. Because... I don't have a cell. Who needs a cell when you only "go" with Natasha, Viktoria or Ivan? And I don't speak Russian; so, I can't call from the apartment phone. There's no computer here to use, no translator website. I can't call the Embassy. I can't tell the Embassy about Ethan!

I can call Dad from the apartment phone using the country code. That piece of paper he gave me…"Keep this with your passport, in your purse pouch-zipped, in case you need it."He firmly instructed with a hug before we left. It's in my purse with the "how to" to call him from Russia. I'll call him and ask him to contact the Embassy about Ethan. I'll ask him to book a flight for us back home.

With a target in my sights, I rush to my purse for the phone number and find the pouch, passport and paper present. As I dial the number, my brain searches for the easiest most effective plan.

Okay, steel yourself for the barrage of questions about leaving before Ethan's status is known. Have the answers ready and deliver them smoothly without hesitation. Don't know what we can do here or how we can help that is my mantra. It makes more sense to work this problem from home. We only have a limited time here, someone is farm sitting for us and someone else is covering Ethan's job. We need to get him out of here asap to get medical treatment. He needs to return to work to keep his job.

As Dad's cell phone rings, I clear my throat and begin shifting my weight from one leg to the next. The dry bitter taste of ash coats my tongue, the same taste left in my mouth after kissing a smoker.

No answer!! It's going to voice mail, and he never checks his voice mail! Maybe, he'll see that I called.

***

Two days of being behind locked doors, to worry, to plot, to be a rock of composure for Zachary, leave me weary and anxious for a phone call—even from Natasha.

"I want to take you to lunch today in Moscow to my favorite restaurant. Viktoria watch Zack for you."

"We be there in an hour."

Surely, she won't want to rumble in front of Viktoria. Although I guess she might, she may be bullying her too. There's no middle class here, only rich or poor and no more. At least, I trust Viktoria with Zachary.

A loud pounding at the door alerts me to their arrival.

With Zack slung over my left shoulder, I unlock the triple locks. Standing aside to let them in, Natasha draped in a floor length mink makes her red carpet entrance, her coat sashaying from side-to-side, the door too small to accommodate such a force of nature. Viktoria follows a few footsteps behind clad in her green wool coat, a small humble smile pasted on her lips.

"Dmitry!" She says as she pulls him away from me. His little fingers dig into my shoulder as he looks at me with teary eyes and a growing frown. His little forehead wrinkles with worry.

He's a person with feelings not a prize in a contest!

"Zack doesn't like to be pulled out of my arms. He likes to make a choice. He'll let you know when he wants to go to you. He'll lean toward you to let you know."

My teeth grit in anger as I stare at her with hate-filled eyes.

"I am mother. I know what they like," she says as she positions him over her shoulder, waving me away. Turning away from me, she looks toward the kitchen.

The room is quiet and still as the clock marks the moments. And in a flash, Zachary screams in full-throated fury as he pushes away from Natasha. Tears stream down his little red face in defiance as he looks at me to rescue him.

What a witch! She doesn't know him.

"All babies aren't the same. I'll take him. I want to say good-bye before we leave." As I move toward him, his arms stretch out to me as he sucks-in his lower lip.

As I hold him over my shoulder, I rub his back lovingly as he sniffles. His little heart races as I kiss his downy head. Finally, his heart slows to match the rhythm of mine—two hearts welded together, separated only by skin and bone.

"I'll be back soon for you, Zachary. Viktoria will take care of you while I'm away," I coo.

With a kiss and a hug, I turn him around to face Viktoria. For a minute or two, he looks at her while she smiles warmly at him. As I slowly inch toward her, he finally leans toward her with his upper body, his legs still laced around my waist. Viktoria reaches for him. With a hug and a back scratch, he smiles for Viktoria.

Okay, he expressed his opinion. All is well.

"Let's go."

So I can get this over with and get you out of our lives, for today.

***

Natasha and I sit in the back of the van looking in opposite directions, like two strangers sharing a bench seat on a city bus. Ivan focuses on the ice and the erratic decisions of the drivers around us. I notice that he doesn't try to make conversation nor check his rear view to look in on us. Buildings reminiscent of a jewelry store case—forgettable white, boring beige and tarnished silver, flank either side of the street. And suddenly, the dazzling blues, greens, pinks and reds of the bejeweled buildings, a juxtaposition of color and grand architecture nestled next to their wretched counterparts. St. Basil's Cathedral appears and glistens in the light, awe-inspiring and delicious. It looks like a confection castle. The cathedral domes stand like swirly soft-serve ice cream coated in M & M shades—of green, blue and red—ready for the taking. An example of peerless architecture that wouldn't be any more extraordinary if made of gingerbread. Of course, some color appears in the form of billboards, signage and tinted windows on some buildings. A blob of Americana anchors street side in the form of McDonalds and Kentucky Fried Chicken, both seductive options at this point. Moscow is the New York City of Russia, buzzing with activity and fueled by an everyday struggle for survival and space. It's New York City with a twist, the New York City in the grip of the Bonanno family when danger and overt corruption became a fixture of daily life just like fighting traffic or shopping at the too busy market.

Sitting in the back of the van with Natasha, I stared in wide-eyed wonder in every direction, a prairie dog not as alert and interested. At the same time that Ivan inches up to the Manhattan-type street side café, I notice turrets at street corners manned by policemen. They brandish their large semi-automatic weapons and keep watch in all directions. The structure of the tower closely resembles a small prison surveillance tower—a vertical iron pillar supporting a cage at the top. Crossing my arms across my chest for more warmth, I study the area. I see them at every turn.

Wonder if those turrets date back to the days of Communism. It's like big brother is always watching. Guess that's a bittersweet story— heavy police presence, good news, probably very necessary, bad news.

Natasha prods me to step out. I stop in my tracks as I catch sight of the entry to the restaurant. Two armed military police stand under the awning on either side of the doorway like bookends at the door. They have machine guns strapped to their bodies which they hold as casually as someone might hold an unwanted overcoat.

As we walk into the restaurant, the toasty warmth, the delicious smells and the chatter of many well-dressed people greet us. An enormous chandelier marks the transition from one world to the other, gritty street side to polished fantasy. The smell of bacon, French Onion soup and filet mignon wafts my way. It reminds me of a photo of a four star restaurant in Paris—white linen tablecloths, sparkling crystal water goblets, walnut chairs and tables, Monet-inspired watercolor landscapes on every crème colored wall, waiters darting hurriedly in starched white shirts, black pants and black aprons balancing trays of savory, steamy food at shoulder level.

One quick Bloody Mary later, I begin to ask questions.

"Why do armed police stand outside this restaurant?"

"For protection of patrons of course," she answers with a roll of her eyes.

Since one side of the restaurant faces the street with a floor to ceiling window, I wonder how much protection the remotely positioned police can provide. After glancing at the Russian/English menu, I order a specialty dish recommended by Natasha—black caviar crepes. The sweet thin crepes arrive housing a bed of salty black caviar, a culinary cream puff masterpiece only a forgotten wallet found containing a stash of cash and pictures would be as delightful.

"Thank you for bringing me here to experience this amazing place. This is the best meal that I've eaten since we've been here."

"Do you have any new information about him?"

"*Da*, he leaves for Vladmir Central in a week. No doctor sees him yet."

"Can you call the American Embassy? It's not something that I can easily do from the apartment. Maybe, Viktoria will call them if you can't."

"Not much you can do. Yes? No computer, no cell phone. You need me," she quips smugly.

I'd like to slap that big smile off her face.

"*Nyet,* the Embassy can't help you. He is criminal until proof innocent."

"I talk to your Dad about work. He say that you try to call him. He ask about you and Ethan. I tell him you good. You miss him. He say he travels to Saudi in a couple of days. He very busy. I tell him I let him know if there is problem."

"You need me," she chuckles as she grabs the check.

And you like that—too much. The phone is my lifeline to leverage, to hope. I wouldn't put it past you to have it disconnected for a while to feed the need and gain more control.

Once again outdoors, I spot a grocery store, point and pull her arm in that direction. At the entryway to the store, more armed guards keep watch outside and inside the store. I search for anything American to satisfy my sense of curiosity. As we browse row after row of products, I grab a small package of American diapers. At a cost of $1 per diaper, I fully realize the economics of not diapering at the child house. After paying for my purchase with a credit card, I skitter past the door sentry for a breath of outdoor air and a sense of space.

Outdoors, I notice several suited men talking with a sentry/military man. In full view of "parking lot; I hear loud, angry conversation; then, the sentry positions himself in the backseat of a nearby vehicle while carefully placing his semi-automatic weapon in his lap. The "suits" fill the remaining space in the Jeep Cherokee before it noisily speeds away.

I don't even want to venture a guess what that's about.

Chapter 32

Back at the apartment, Natasha goes to the kitchen to take a business call. Zack sleeps in the bedroom. Viktoria grabs her coat and gloves to leave. I move close to her while keeping my eyes on the entrance to the kitchen. I whisper.

"Viktoria, please, please take this number and call my Dad. Tell him we need help—HIS HELP. Ask him to call the Embassy about Ethan. The Embassy must know about this. Ask him to call me, not Natasha. No one will ever know you called—I promise. We can tell Natasha, if asked, that it was my Dad's idea."

While slipping the scrap of paper into her gloved hand, Natasha walks back into the room—shaking her head, her lips hard and tight.

Quickly, I look at the floor.

Did it fall on the floor? Or is it in her hand? Did Natasha see or hear anything?

Seeing nothing on the floor, I breathe a sigh of relief. Glancing at Viktoria's eyes, I see her face turned to stone, frozen in thought.

Will she chose allegiance to Natasha or do the right thing? Is that a small smile she's struggling to hide? Maybe, she sees a chance for some payback.

Natasha stops, hands on hips facing us, her eyes bouncing from Viktoria to me and back again, a painted scowl on her face.

"Now, what do I miss?"

She seems engaged but disengaged. Her eyes are looking beyond us. She's still wrapped up in that phone call. It's time to change the subject and get rid of them.

"Just thanking Viktoria for taking good care of Zack. She mentioned that he's still congested. He's improving, but it's a slow process. I'll call Dad and ask him to call the doctor. Maybe, I need to change the dosage on his meds."

"Stupid! You, Americans and your drugs! Onions and mustard poultice cure him quickly! Poor baby suffer for your bad decisions!" She snarls.

I can handle this. Stay cool! Subject changed. Viktoria out of the line of fire and scrutiny.

"We'll see how he does the next couple of days and talk about it," I say with forced pleasantness, my nostrils flaring in disgust.

"I'm tired. I'm sure we can continue this later. Do you need to grab anything before you leave?" This time the pleasant demeanor comes easily.

* * *

Later that day, Natasha calls.

"Zack must have passport photos. It will only take a few minutes and I'll bring him back to the apartment."

"What? Ethan isn't with us yet. It doesn't seem necessary right now."

Actually, this will make it easier to leave when we make those arrangements, but she expects me to argue. It's more convincing.

"Why now?" I ask, my brows arching in wonder.

"Because time is good for me now. You need it, and you need me to help."

"Is Ivan driving you? How long will it take? Will you have the pictures immediately?" I dig in.

With a roll of her eyes punctuated by a sigh, she answers sharply.

"Yes, one hour and yes."

"Well, then, okay, but I want to hand Zack to Ivan to carry to the van since he doesn't like being yanked around by you; that way, he won't be screaming all the way to van."

Thank God for Benadryl. It'll be easier for Zack.

When Natasha returns, she prances toward me.

"Here are the official photos plus a few extras," she says.

I look at the extras, one depicts her in a Madonna pose lovingly looking at Zack while the other captures a content Natasha holding him in her lap, both of them facing the lens.

"Do you mind?" She asks innocently as I look at the pictures.

What is she thinking? Does she think we want to immortalize her in our family photo albums? She didn't even ask if she could take extra pictures with him. Those poses are inappropriate for a non-parent. It's crossing the line of paid assistant in this situation. I don't know if we want pictures of him in her hands... I'm sure she kept extras for herself.

"Actually, I do mind. I can't wait till he goes home with us," I smirk. I bury my anger in a half-smile as my maternal instincts battle with my rational thoughts.

I'm trying to think big picture with this small picture situation, but it can come back to haunt him. Does she plan to knock on his door with pictures in hand and invite herself into his life later? She travels to the US on a regular basis. I'll insure that he gets to invite into his life whomever he wants. There will be no implicit endorsement card played here via association with my father or by virtue of being a Russian involved in the process. It will always be his choice. That will be one of my guarantees to him.

The gotcha smile plays on her lips. The smile that says "You're wrong about me and kids. Here's proof."

"I'll make toilet then leave."

As she walks to the bathroom, I walk to the kitchen on a mission.

I can't wait to dispose of these.

I tear the extras into small pieces and throw them in the kitchen trash, dumping yesterday's wadded tissues and the morning coffee grinds onto the pile. Turning back toward the entryway, a smile of radiant joy marks my triumph.

Okay, change. Here she comes. Be perturbed.

"I call you later," she waves me away, dismissively as if swatting away a fly.

After closing and locking the door behind her, I go to the bathroom to check the medicine cabinet. The smell in the room is noxious like rotting trash.

She didn't flush the toilet.

The ugly sight of bloody water and floating poo makes me hold my nose, turn away and gag. Turning back to flush the toilet with the pull chain, I notice a piece of string.

I can't flush this because her tampon will probably clog the pipes. This is DISGUSTING! Accident or not? Regardless, I've got to fish that out to flush.

Going back to the kitchen, I grab a large straining spoon and the trash, towing it behind me. Holding my breath, I fish out the tampon and place it carefully on top of the coffee grinds, and flush the toilet. With great care, I twist and knot the trash liner. I tote the bag to the front door, unlock it and open it. With one big heave, I hurl it toward the stairs.

Chapter 33

Tossing and turning, I finally give up on my hope for sleep. Since I haven't really slept in days, I check the clock—hoping I logged a few hours.

It's midnight here; so, probably, noon in the US. My thoughts revert to Dad and how he'd take charge.

Dad, please call me. There's so much to do, to worry about. It's overwhelming! The priority is Ethan; then, us. Ethan's arm could require amputation at this point. Dad always said "Don't worry about things you can't control."

Got to dig deep like I did after the riding accident. Got to be strong, focus on the positive. Got to leverage everything within reach! Hopefully, Viktoria helps me. And Natasha. What's going on with her? The bathroom, the bullying, the… the blood on her face…the blood that matted her hair. Got to study that, figure it out and use it somehow.

***

Someone is pulling my hair. Is this the dream in which I think I'm awake? Did I fall asleep? Where's Zack?

With a start, I wake-up. Zack's hand coils in my hair, tugging to get my attention.

Sitting up, I scoop him up and kiss his hands and head. He grabs my chin and squeezes.

He always makes me smile. He's perfection in this polar prison.

"Okay, I get it. It's breakfast time." Grabbing his little hand, I gently tap the tip of his nose smiling indulgently, sunbeams of happiness warming the moment.

A peek at the clock quickens my pace.

"Wow! Both of us slept late. It's nine o'clock."

Like we can go anywhere, do much of anything, like we have to be somewhere. BUT we can enjoy each other. And that is exactly what I plan to do!

After breakfast, I play horsey for Zack to proudly sit on and lie on, my hair reins that I never knew existed. A short time later, we sit on the couch while I read a book to him. The *tick tock* of the clock interrupted suddenly.

Knock, knock.

Someone is at the door. No one is supposed to be here now. They always call.

I freeze statue-still and listen again before giving Zack a binky and putting him on the bed with his red and white toy.

While walking to the door quietly, I notice the knocking stops.

Standing at the door, I cock my head to use my ear at closer range, leaning into the door.

Is someone still there? They probably heard me reading to Zack. Do I open the door?

No, I need to stand here and figure this out. Neighbor or mafia? No, the neighbors are probably scared and private. And the Mafia would shoot through the locks.

Looking down, I stroke my chin with my forefinger, the wheels of analysis rotating quickly like the tires of a speeding car.

The answer is in front of you.

A snippet of white catches my eye—white on the floor at the door… white under the door…rammed under the edge of the door… half of it in the room. Sitting down on the floor, I begin to take a closer look.

It's an envelope! Can I pull it through?

I tug at it, gently like it's an explosive device. Looks smooth not chunky. Dirt smudges on the right side.

Closing my eyes to focus, I run my semi-clamped forefinger and thumb across the half of the envelope. My mind reverts from threat to detective mode.

No metal, no wires. Crinkling means paper, letter size. I bet it's a note! Don't smell it! Just examine it for now.

By carefully pulling, I thread the note through.

As I rip it open and unfold it, my eyes dart to the end of the page.

It's from Viktoria!

Sophia,

I will help you and your family if you promise protection through your Dad. It will all be his idea. You are correct about the phone-she disconnected it this morning. Ivan told me. He worries about her. She is different, angry and aggressive. Ivan thinks her 20-year-old brother is hurting her again. He lives with her. He has no job. He drinks and does not like being around people. He plays games all day. She won't let the Government help him. She is his only living family. She says she is responsible for him.

I called your Dad. He is calling the Embassy. He wants me to check on you; so, we make signals. You put something red in the window if you are in trouble. I'll find something for you to use. I'll see it when I drive by. I will drive by everyday at noon. I will try to get you and the baby out of here safely.

Viktoria

Chapter 34

So, her brother beats her. That's sad, but it doesn't justify her rough treatment toward me. I don't like for her to be around Zack as unpredictable as she is. Maybe, I can make sure that he's tired and ready for a nap when she arrives. She always calls and gives me some notice, but now without a phone...Oh! I hope Zack wasn't exposed to her brother when she took him for photos. Probably not! She probably has more sense than that, cares for Zack more than that.

Do I let her bully me? Do I create more problems to keep her focus off Zack?

Taking the note, I walk to the stove and hold it over the burner until it flames—holding it over the sink until it singes my fingertips. Taking the remaining bit of note, I water it down and wash it down the sink, letting the garbage disposal digest the rest.

Now, what?

The drum beat of multiple plastic objects slamming into a wall then crashing onto the floor answers my question—it's Zack time.

***

It's been two days since Viktoria's note and no word from Natasha. Sitting at the kitchen table, I scribble on a piece of paper as some mindless dribble plays softly on the radio. Zack naps in the bedroom.

I guess stewing in ignorance has to be a way of life for us! I frown bitterly as the thought rips across my brain.

It's one of those days—beyond bad, beyond blizzard. A day I'd choose to stay in, to flirt and snuggle with Ethan. A day custom-made for welding our bodies together, my she melting into his he, followed by a feast of chips and velvety cheesy hot sauce. Of course, an adventure action film marathon backdrop would add to the perfection. We'd argue about the next twist and turn in the plot line; then, wrestle and knot together once again. The sensational sex with him is better than teenage post-accident sex with Luke, by far. But what a great memory that was…

On a sunny afternoon when we had my house to ourselves, I wanted to be a good girl, but the bad girl got in the way. The" games" began poolside in our swimsuits…

***

"Do you want something to drink?" I ask like a good hostess; yet, I'm talking to his chest. My eyes and attention focus on his chest as if it's a chocolate fudge sheet cake, and I need a chocolate fix.

I can't believe that I'm talking to his chest. I hope my eyes aren't glazed with desire.

"Sophia, why not linger a while? I can make you smolder if you give me the chance." he says with a mischievous grin as he grabs my hand, kissing the top of it and the underside of my wrist.

I like that.

I savor it a few seconds, while gazing at his dreamy attentive face, before I pull it away. There's just something about Luke…

"Like I said how about that drink?" I wink.

I want him but not his way, my way. Exactly on my terms.

I stroll into the house taking his eyes with me. I grab two cans of Sprite. No liquor will distort this experience and maximize my penalty if Mom comes home early.

What now? Step two-drive him crazy with desire.

I pop the pull tabs and walk purposefully outside.

A sheet of diamond dust partially covers the pool. Five-foot Palm trees planted in each corner of the rectangular backyard add to the tropical ambience.

Luke steps in front of me as I walk out of the sliding glass door. He takes his drink and mine and sets it on the pass-through window counter next to the sliding glass door. He turns back to me and closes the sliding glass door behind me holding my gaze the entire time. Then, he puts his hands on the door above my shoulders and leans into me, closing his eyes and brushing his lips lightly against mine.

I'm loving that! What a tease! He's going to make it tough for me to hang on to my... resolve. I'm afraid to know, but I've got to know.

I open my eyes slowly and focus on not puckering my lips. He stands upright before me, fighting back a smile. He gently takes my hand, kisses the back of it, and then places it on his cheek. He takes my other hand covering it with his and puts in on his heart.

How romantic! I'm faltering. Remember to make this my game! I look at him with soft eyes and smile mildly, struggling with my screaming hormones. I dare a glance down.

Oh, no, he's so muscled, that hairy chest and those abs! Abs as seductive as tucked satin sheets, soft yet firm. Sheets that I want to touch and stroke lightly and brush my face across. Suddenly, I realize that I was grazing my hands along his abs, moving my hands softly up and down the symmetrical halves of his marbled stomach.

My hands are in the chocolate cake. Retreat quickly! Change the subject to rein myself in.

I retract my hand in surprise—the touch of a hot stove no hotter than those abs.

I pull his hand back toward me and put it on my cheekbone. Then, I drag his index finger slowly across my upper and then lower lip tracing each curvature. He gasps, pulls his hand back and takes a deep controlled breath as if he had touched a sizzling skillet.

Luke combs my hair back away from the side of my face with his hands. He turns my face toward his and kisses me lightly and slowly—just a feathery touch of his lips that leaves me hungry for more. He smiles as he hears my irregular breath. There's more teasing over and over again with chaste gentle glancing kisses. His left hand burrows in my hair above my ear and the right plays conductor to the orchestra of sensations raging under his touch.

He moves his fingers to my lips and lets them glide to my chin to the hollow in my neck between my collarbones. He leans into me and kisses me there—a chaste kiss then a French kiss. My flushed face is now cupped in between his hands—wanton for more attention like a piece of clay waiting for the sculptor's next thought. He stops for a moment and gazes at me. His smile looks playful and controlled like he'd just captured my knight in a game of chess. His eyes sparkle with dreamy radiance.

He's masterful at this game. The girls were right.

Oh, my gosh, my pelvis and breasts are pulsating. I won't let him hear me moan.

I put my hands on top of his and guided them from my face to my neck to the bikini straps on my shoulders as he kisses the sides of my neck.

He stops mid-kiss.

I press his hands on the straps in a downward motion over my shoulders. He slow kisses a trail from my upper to my lower lip to my neck to my shoulder. I lean into him pressing myself like cookie dough into a mould.

Ohhhhh…. Advantage me.

"You'd better stop there or I'll lose my mind." he whispers.

Game on! I've got him now.

"Luke, I want to feel your skin against mine. All of your skin."

With a sigh, he tilts his head and looks at me if I'd flashed my breasts. He longs to have me. His eyes are lit. He smiles slowly and seductively. The victory of winning our game, or so he thinks, reflects in his eyes and his dirty smile. He scoops me up and carries me upstairs to my room.

He's never seen my room—a big rectangular shape with two medium sized picture windows which overlook the street—a watchtower for traffic in and out of the house. My twin bed with the white leather headboard and inlaid flower prints is in the center between the picture windows. Two red, blue and white pom poms framed a poster of a lion hang above the bed between the windows. A picture of two handsome leading men, in a Western movie that I recently saw, hangs on the wall adjacent from my bed and above my bookshelf. The walls are snow white. Another bookshelf with a stereo system leans on the other adjacent wall. The sheets and comforter on my bed add the most color to the room, designer sheets in white with random long stem thorn less yellow roses scattered throughout. The comforter and pillowcase are soft and match the sheets.

"I know this will be good for me, but honestly, I want it to be good for you. You've been through hell. I owe this to you. I've thought about being with you since the day we met. You've been in my dreams a lot." Hearing the honesty in his voice, I look into his too committed, covetous eyes and see that he adores me.

He carefully places me on my bed with a smile. He lies next to me propped up on one elbow and gazes down at me as I lie flat on my back.

"Tell me what you want. My bad judgment almost killed you. Anything you want, any way you want. I've wanted to be right here right now for you for a long time. I've dreamed and thought about it for a long time." He leans into me and swallows hard. He stares at me with soft sincere eyes and then moves his lips lightly against mine—an almost non kiss, a slow touch. Then, he moves his scratchy face gently across my right cheekbone as he kisses my earlobe. I gasp as his face brushes mine.

His scratchy face feels wonderful against me. I'm so into this…

"I can wait and control myself. I'm always prepared. Anything, Sophia. Anything," he leans over, whispering in my ear. He slowly strokes my cheekbone with his curled fingers. I hear his words and feel his warm breath. I smell his woodsy fresh air cologne and his Sprite-drenched mouth.

I pull him to my face and whisper back into his ear.

"Luke, you're so amazing and so sexy. I hunger for you. I love what you're doing. It's perfect, romance novel perfect. Every second is pleasure," I tell him as I playfully nibble his neck.

He smiles confidently as he gazes at my face. He leans over me. Long sighs and loud breathing fill the room. Slow gentle kisses on my lips, kiss trails down my neck, nibbles and suction and back to my lips again. A kiss trail and a nibble from my lower lip to my chin to the hollow of my neck. As he kisses my collarbone to shoulder, he pushes my bikini straps down further. As he runs the back of his hand along the top portion of my bikini top, I exhale loudly. After he traces the vertical line that separates my abs from my tight midriff, he kisses underneath my still clinging bikini top. I felt his hot breath and the dull sandpaper edge to his face. He runs his hand along the inside of my thighs as if trying to feel every skin cell. I comb my hands through his hair. I'm stunned and dazed.

This is scary and wonderful. I have to know …

Gentler teasing, a light kiss on my parted lips—deliberate and controlled. I grab handfuls of hair on either side of his face and pull him closer, returning his light kisses with scorching caged desire. My whole body tingles, and I want him. I put my arms around his waist and run my nails along his back roughly. I never felt more like an animal than now—my pupils feel dilated, my breathing is loud and ragged, and my heart is racing.

He pulls my greedy hands away and waives his index finger at me like he's scolding a naughty pet.

"Not yet. Extraordinary, remember?" He glows as he raises his eyebrows and smiles.

More kisses along the trails, now both gentle and passionate. A never-ending approach and retreat that leaves me breathless. And wildfire intensity that won't be denied any longer.

Hands knitted together and frayed, sheets disheveled and a comforter fallen to the floor—the physical release of marathoners finishing an important race and the cool satisfying spray of a fountain on overheated skin.

Our bodies blush as if sunburned red, dotted with beads of sweat like sprinkles on cupcakes. My relaxed happy body satiated by his adoring beautiful face and stroked by his patient educated lips and hands.

And I know I'll be okay.

I'll be just fine.

***

Standing at the window, I look out at the snow, savoring my memories of unbridled joy and triumph over a tragic twist in my life. In a flash, my thoughts turn.

Sex with Ethan will be different now. The playful domination will have to change. Ponytail ruined that for me, for us. The bad girl needs time to process all of that. It'll have to be like it was with Luke, adoring and attentive. I'm so lonely…I feel like such a slut, thinking about Luke now when Ethan is in prison.

Sex! I wonder if Ethan is being coerced into sex. He has to be in that prison by now. I can't go there—it's too dark! Wait! Maybe, just maybe, the injury will isolate him and protect him from the general population for a while. If he can't function, they'd almost have to treat him.

Hopefully, he's better off than I thought. Like a Morning glory curled around a gate, I cling to that.

Chapter 35

Another day rolls by as I wait for someone to contact me. Zack and I are sitting on the couch, playing peek-a-boo when I hear rustling at the door.

I'm betting it's Natasha's full length mink coat.

"Be a good boy for me, Zack and play with toys on the bed. Mommy has to talk to someone." I mutter as I carry him into the bedroom.

"Your phone not working, but I have news for you. Let me in!" She shouts as she pounds the door.

Good Grief! Is there a fire?

Waltzing in, her eyes search for Zack; then, she looks at me like I'm the impertinent door man. Her red silk low-cut shirt and black wool pants are a mix of hot and dark.

Just like me, hot with anger and dark with an agenda—to keep her at a distance and escape.

I sneer, moving my hand quickly to cover my "sudden" need to cough.

"Okay…" I murmur, looking above her head.

"Ethan is at Vladmir Central now. They treat his wound since the Embassy tell them he is a political prisoner. Reports are they cut a piece to prevent spread of infection. Your Dad contact

Embassy and hire investigator. He thinks he can prove Ethan not guilty."

"That's the best! The best news! I yell, finally, a touchdown thrill in a lopsided game.

I notice Natasha chooses to ignore my sudden burst of happiness.

"How?"

"The investigator believes that he can get the video from the bar that night. Do you remember the date?"

"Yes," I tell her. I wish I could forget, but it's burned in my brain. It was November 25th which is an important date in America."

"I will tell him. Now, I want to hold Zack."

"Wait!" I extend my arm out to her, my hand spread to stop her motion.

"How does the investigator think he can get the video?" I quiz.

With a roll of her eyes and a this-is-a-waste of my time frown, she explains.

"The Mafia make surveillance tapes of bar every day. They do this for many reasons—keep people true and to find new marks for biz."

My brain begins to weld together the information.

An employee would lie to the Mafia? Or cheat the Mafia? Risky, but it happens in the US with rival groups. No reason it wouldn't be possible here.

Marks for biz? That must mean trolling for targets for robbery, prostitution or ... scapegoats for their crimes.

"Wouldn't they keep those tapes secure, locked away?" My face feels like a slideshow of emotions—sad, hopeful, tentative and happy that there's a chance for exoneration.

"No, they are Mafia. No one interested in stealing those tapes from them. Thieves only interested in cash, money, jewelry. He thinks they'll be in a box in the bar," She says evenly.

Yes! Finally, I have an anchor for hope and optimism. What an angle! My smile is irrepressible, refusing to drown in dark thoughts. Ripples of relaxation wash over me as I soak in the warm memories of holding Ethan in my arms.

"Now, back to Zack. I want to see him."

Here we go again, back to the grind of dealing with Natasha.

"I'll go check on him to see if he's asleep," I offer. As I walk toward the bedroom, I feel her eyes following my every step. A loud *thud* answers my question as Zack hurls a toy at the wall. In the doorway, he sees me, greeting me first with a giggle then a spray of raspberry. I nod my head as the can't-be-denied smile returns.

He couldn't be more perfect! I love him so! And I won't let her make him cry!

As I lean over the bed, he reaches his arms out to me. Hoisting him into my arms, I inch my way into the next room—floating in a stormy sea of thoughts.

Need to figure out how to manage this. How? How?

I've got to temper my actions. I know a mother is one of the most dangerous creatures on earth. Like it or not, I may need her. But she is untrustworthy. I see it and feel it.

As I walk toward her, I feel his once soft heavy body turn to concrete. And I know exactly what I must do.

As we enter the room, she bounds across the distance separating us—her arms outstretched. Her eyes laser-in on Zack, like a guided missile. He squirms and buries his head in my neck, his binky scratching my neck with ever-increasing rhythm like a woodpecker on a tree in relentless pursuit of pecking gratification.

"Wait! He's been sick, and he may make you sick," I lie.

"I do not care! I want to hold him!" She cries as she lunges toward him, wrenching him from my arms. Rivers of lava churn through my veins as I'm forced to let go. I see the volcano erupting as his binky falls to the floor.

I'm not playing tug-of-war with my baby!

"Stop! Give him back to me! He doesn't like to be grabbed!" I hiss.

"Zack, I love you. I want baby!" she cries out as he screams in fury. Tears stream from his cheeks. His bottom lip quivers as he gasps for air.

"I said give him back to me now! He's still sick and now upset!" I shriek. "Think about him. It's not just about you!" I glare with the ferocity of a momma bear, my heart full of adrenaline and anger.

Tears mist her eyes as he reaches his arms out for me.

As I take him from her, I notice her red silk shirt is wet, wet over her breasts. Black and blue fingerprints dot her neck ineptly camouflaged by pancake foundation. A hickey peeks out from the top of her bra.

Oh my, she's fighting a lot of problems. How sad! She's producing milk for Zack. She's way too involved, but I need the info about Ethan. We need her help. I must walk a line between white-hot hate and cool compromise. Bet this wouldn't have happened with an adoption specialist rather than a conscripted never-done-it-before, never-will-do-it-again company executive. Oh, well. It is what it is... A sigh escapes my lips as I study Natasha's face.

"Maybe, you should take a different approach. Talk to him or play with him. Don't just grab him like he's your mink coat. Be respectful of his space and opinions," I advise sincerely.

Turning away from me, she wipes away her tears and veers toward the door as a weathered slouching wreck of a woman.

Before she exits, she turns to me.

"I want baby, but boyfriend says no. He not let me have one," she sputters.

I hope her rotten boyfriend treats her better than her brother does. How could a boyfriend allow that? Is she dealing with two abusive men or could her rotten "boyfriend" be her brother?

***

I must be more understanding. I have to be always aware of her hardship. Wish I'd known this pre-trip. You never know what's going on in someone's life. How can she even stay hinged? I shudder at the thought of two abusive men in her life.

Two days pass as I wait for the next visitor. A visitor brings information while enjoying the company of another adult is irrelevant.

At noon, a knock at the door as a note slides under the door.

> *I try to get information for you about Ethan. It may be too difficult to try to help him at this time. I would not keep my hopes high. You're in a bad situation I know, but be patient. Maybe, I can get someone to help me help you. The Embassy told your Dad that Americans who commit crimes have to pay the price. Sorry the news is bad.*
> *Viktoria*

After reading it twice, I crumple it, and burn it over the stove, but that isn't enough. I grab the damp dishtowel, lying on the counter, to wipe away the remaining ashes. As I rinse the towel, I watch the gray ashes circle the drain before they disappear.

Chapter 36

Tossing and turning in bed, my mind ricochets from one question to the next.

Could Viktoria have an agenda too? What could she possibly want?

Looking at the clock, I see that it's 3 am, I've been trying to sleep since midnight.

So far, there's been no reason to distrust Viktoria, but Natasha…

Of course, I interact more with Natasha.

I have to remember that false hope is the worst agony. Have to try to remember not to bury myself in worry about things over which I have no control. It could drive me to drink. Need to find out how and when we can get out of here. Need answers about Viktoria.

"Groceries!"

It's the first step. I have a plan.

Bolting out of bed, I throw aside the covers. After switching on the lamp, I rummage through Zack's clothes, looking for a red sock or shirt.

Grabbing two socks, I tie them together and hang them in the window.

***

It's 12:30. She'll be here soon.

We're sitting on the couch watching no-TV TV. I mute the sound since I can't understand the language anyway. Water boils in the kitchen for tea or for whatever else I may need it for.

Someone is fumbling with a key and the doorknob turns.

"Shhhh......Zack," I instruct holding my finger to my lips.

Viktoria peeks around the door, like a furtive fox peeking around a tree.

Spotting us on the couch, her jaw drops in bewilderment.

I smile and wave her in, putting Zack on the floor with his toys. I walk toward her, looking at her square in the eyes.

"What's so important!" she spits.

"We need food and supplies. It's hard to exist with what little we have. Natasha and I didn't talk about that problem the last time we saw her. Will you mention it to Ivan or Natasha that we are running low on supplies now?" I ask. "Know Dad would want that."

"Yes, of course. Now, I must go."

"One last thing, I'm heartbroken after reading your note about Ethan. Is there any hope?" I whine.

"No, I do not believe so," I notice her eyes meet mine briefly.

"Are you sure about the information?"

"Yes, again, of course," she answers, her voice thick with irritation.

Now, she's looking through me.

"Why do you think Natasha would disconnect the phone? It's not like we can use it anyway."

"She is very strange now. Who knows?"

Her arms cross over her chest as the boiling water in the kitchen calls to me.

With a quick glance over my shoulder at Zack, I walk to the stove.

Hmmmm... She's lying and she's nervous.

"Would you like some tea?" I offer as I gaze at her, teapot in hand.

"No, thank you."

That's when I see it—the glint of worry in her eyes.

***

It's early evening, when loud rustling at the door alerts me to Natasha's presence.

"It me, Natasha. Please open door," she asks as she energetically pounds at the door with her fist.

Zack sits propped up in my lap enjoying his bottle at the kitchen table. Rising slowly from the chair, I re-position him over my shoulder, replacing the bottle with the always nearby binky.

Sweeping into the room, Natasha carries two sacks of groceries.

Okay, now, I may get somewhere.

"Viktoria call me and say you need more supplies now."

"I forgot to mention that earlier. Glad to have the supplies. Thank you."

With a smile, Natasha walks quickly to the kitchen and begins to unpack the bags near the drain board.

Standing at the sink, I hoist Zack on my hip while leaning back against the counter.

No crying, the energy is good.

"I need to check when phone be fixed. It taking much time. Then, you can call me and let me know that you need something."

What! It is Viktoria! She's lying like I thought.

My jaw drops as my knees buckle. And another heavy weight locks into place on my shoulders.

I must rely on two liars for help with Ethan. And I must rely on two liars to return safely to the States. Why would Viktoria lie to me? What can she possibly want—ransom? How can she disconnect the phone?

Zack cries and the energy is now different. Natasha stares at me, her face frozen in shock.

She knows…She knows that I suspect her of being the reason…

"Why do you think I do something like this?" She hisses, her fists balling at her sides in anger.

"Zack, you need to go to bed for a few minutes while Mommy talks to Natasha. Ok? I'll come to get you soon."

I kiss him on the top of his head as he nuzzles into my neck, dousing it with tears. As I walk to the bedroom, I grab his red and white toy on the way.

When I lean over the bed, his arms grip more tightly around my neck. Scratching his back and rocking him gently before I put him on the bed with his toy, I smile and kiss each little finger on his hands.

"I love you, Zack. Be back to get you soon."

Walking backward and waving good-bye, I exit the room, holding my breath in fear that he'll begin crying.

"You know… I've been locked in this apartment for days at a time—separated from Ethan, worrying about Ethan. I don't know what to think," I say, squaring my shoulders and studying her with a murderous stare.

Truthfully, I think Viktoria bribed someone to disconnect the phone and told you there was a problem with the line. If someone can buy a college degree, someone can bribe a phone company employee. It seems reasonable that you'd give her the number for communication purposes with us. After all, she is the translator.

"Just wondering... Does Viktoria have the apartment phone number?"

"Da, yes, of course," she answers evenly. Her eyes bifocal in size as she comes to the same realization that I do—Viktoria has a hidden motive.

Nervously, she grabs her coat and gloves, heading for the door.

"I must consider this and talk to you tomorrow."

She's upset that she's made a mistake in hiring a translator. She's upset that everything just became more dangerous in Moscow, already one of the most dangerous cities in the world.

"Wait! Is there any news about Ethan?" I plead.

"Yes, the investigator found the tape. He make copies and send to the US Embassy to secure Ethan's release. We hope he free in a few days."

"It's the best—the best of news!" I shout like a giddy grand prize-winner in a sweepstakes.

"Before I go, your Dad and Sergei need me. You still need me to complete final work before you leave. If Viktoria wants to do something bad, it's not guilt on me. I check with some people and let you know about the phone," she adds anxiously.

My thoughts, once scattered, now flying in formation like ducks traveling to a different location to roost.

The phone is not a worry now. Intent is the only worry. The phone can't help me if there's a sudden problem. What exactly does she want? How do I protect us?

***

Rummaging, looking for items for defense. My brain gears into overdrive as I assemble an arsenal. And there are no matches, no drain cleaner and no guns.

Things will happen fast once Natasha starts asking questions at the phone company.

Ah… finally, a lighter and a sharp butcher knife, in the top drawer of the kitchen next to the silverware tray. I snatch it vowing to carry it close at all times.

Next, I search the bathroom. I hit the jackpot! I find pills, a bottle of alcohol, bleach, a few razor blades and a can of hair spray. I grab the razor blades, bleach, hair spray and alcohol.

Now, I just need a plan—several of them.

Chapter 37

What did I expect—a night of peaceful slumber?

Groggy with sleeplessness, I stumble out of bed and check the clock. It's 6 am, and my brain burns from fatigue. Zack sleeps soundly while I smile lovingly at him and worry. Grabbing the flashlight I found yesterday, I look for a path away from the bed.

Now, I have an arsenal of tools—a bottle of alcohol, bleach, razor blades, hairspray, a butcher knife and a lighter.

No match for a gun, but a wedge of hope for us. Now, where to put them and how to best use them?

In the kitchen, I start a pan of tea, not a pot.

A pan is a more useful tool for defense than a pot. I'll say it's just an old habit if asked. I'll keep a pan of water on the stove, ready to boil. As I poke around in the cupboards, I find a long slender water pitcher. I can use that.

I sit at the kitchen table and map strategically located hiding places for my weapons—the entryway, the kitchen, the bedroom and the bathroom. Systematically, I analyze every angle, every scenario.

The bathroom is a little too obvious and too comfortable for cornering someone. It's the perfect location for blocking access to food and the front door.

An entry table and lamp flank the door on one side. There's an expanse of wall on the other side. The wall ends at a corner followed by a coat closet and the bathroom.

Grabbing the lamp, I upend it looking for a hollow space.

Lots of space here! Need to make it stick. Need....tissue or toilet paper to wrap my weapon.

Snatching the paper from the bathroom, I'm back at the entryway, twisting the mummified lighter and razor blade into the lamp. I add an extra measure of paper to insure it's anchored.

Now, the alcohol... The bottle should be in the entry table drawer.

Okay, done...I'll put the hairspray there too.

The kitchen...where knives and cutting are expected. The pan of tea and the bleach kept in the bathroom may be the answer here.

The bleach....Where do I put the bleach?

Grabbing the water pitcher, I open the top and fill it almost full, putting it on the counter next to Zack's clean bottles.

Check! Now, the bedroom... a knife and a razor blade. I can hit with the flashlight too. Need to protect Zack from this stuff. I'll put it under the mattress where I sleep. The flashlight stays on the floor on my side.

Walking to the bathroom carrying a roll of tape, I slowly survey the area around me. All high-traffic areas include a covert attack tool. A wicked smile takes shape on my lips that suddenly reverts to a frown as I enter the bathroom.

By taping one end of the blades to make them manageable for slashing, I can place them under the stack of hand towels. I search the room again for a spray, maybe a room freshener or anti-bacterial spray.

Voici! An aerosol can labeled with a picture of a roach! Roach spray! All in one room—towels to shield my arms plus spray and blades. This is my last resort room, the last place I'd want to be since I don't have a gun. The rumbling boil of water reminds me it's time to sit, to drink and to plot.

In the kitchen, I find cold cuts and beets to satisfy my hunger, and I begrudgingly eat every bite.

***

We're playing with toy cars on the floor, one zipping by the next when I hear a rustling at the door.

Natasha!

In a flash, I'm up on my feet—ready to answer her knock at the door. Leaning over, I extend my arms for Zack, who accepts my invitation. His toothless smile makes my heart flutter.

"It is Natasha. Please open door!" She shouts as if I may be in the next room.

One nano second later, I open the door to wave her in. As usual, she zeros-in on Zack.

"There he is… my favorite baby in world," she exclaims.

This time, she smiles widely, holding her arms out for him.

Leaning his upper body toward her and away from me, he acknowledges the question and goes into her arms.

"That's what I want!" She squeaks.

I notice her gripping him too tightly like a python squeezing a mouse. Zack squirms and pushes away with his arms, his face twisting in irritation. Natasha immediately relaxes her arms.

Finally, she listened.

Good, for both of them! He can tolerate her fawning over him this way.

"I've got more news for you. Ivan tell me Viktoria has money problems. She may have plan for you and the baby that you don't like."

"What do you suggest I do besides sit here like a caged animal?" I snap.

"I can't take you to my house. You don't want to go there. My brother is …. not well. At Ivan's house, lots of visitors. It not safe when you can't speak Russian. It's too bad. You stay here," she says as her smile defies her sense of empathy.

Shifting Zack to her right shoulder, I watch her run her finger along the length of the entry table.

"*Da,* that would be tough. You don't have choices. Do you?"

I glare as Natasha beams.

She can potentially gain from my misfortune too, that's not lost on her. Collaboration may be part of the plan. Bitch!

"Any news about Ethan?" I ask, afraid of the answer. My body tenses in pain as I speak his name like a cord too tightly stretched starting to fray.

"Much papervork. Not yet. More days," she reports.

"Won't money speed-up the process?"

"*Da,* it is."

Translation: I have to deal with Viktoria alone. One against one or one against two.

"What do I do to protect myself?"

"Well, that is not problem for me. Is it?" She snaps.

"I can tell my boss I help you a lot now."

Collaboration, it wouldn't be about money for Natasha, it would be about Zack. Viktoria is probably not interested in Zack. What could she do with him? Try to re-adopt him for money? That's too complicated when ransom would be so much easier.

"Thanks for stopping by. I'm tired and want to rest with Zack."

Extending my arms out for Zack, he replies in our unspoken language by leaning toward me.

Before releasing him, Natasha holds him in a tight embrace, kissing him on the head. He squirms, his lips forming a frown as he sucks in his lower lip.

"He's about to cry. I think he's ready for a nap too," I kindly insist.

"Good-bye!" She shouts as she slams the door behind her.

Definitely, unstable.

***

It's a new day, a day closer to dangerous life-changing events. It's still dark outside as I peek at the clock, the neon green numbers show 2 am. I rub my eyes and check-in on Zack. He looks so angelic and peaceful as he sleeps. I lace my hands behind my head. It's so quiet I can hear myself breathe. My demons gather to taunt me now via my thoughts.

Viktoria's visit is imminent. This is exhausting! Got to focus on what's going right! Ethan, being released, and Zack thriving. Even if I don't make it, Dad and Ethan will never give up on Zack.

And then, the sound of rustling and a click at the front door.

Sirens scream in my brain.

I move closer to Zack, pulling the mattress along with me. Using my other arm, I feel for the stash of weapons—roach spray, knife, razor blades and flash light.

Adrenaline floods my body as I drop the mattress to grab the spray and knife. I glance at Zack to hard wire his beautiful presence in my memory. Adrenaline, a tsunami now, topping the floodgates as I lie still, waiting for the faint silhouette in the bedroom doorway to make a move. My hand twitches on the roach spray trigger. My fingers flex and release on the knife.

Yes, I'm ready to kill, to fight to the death.

I must be still. I must act asleep. I must wait for this person to close-in on me. I dare not move, my eyes slits. I try to memorize everything about the person in the doorway, my heart battering the inside wall of my chest.

The street lights streaming beams of light, revealing a patchwork quilt of light and dark. The person, in the doorway, re-adjusts his erect posture and leans his back against the inner doorframe—a spider in waiting sprawled out on a web of intricate design. A cherry fireball dangles from the fingers of his left hand.

Now, I see teeth, lots of them forming a smile. Slow and measured, this faceless person takes a deep hit off the cigarette. His breath hisses as he tilts his head upward, releasing the smoke toward the ceiling. An eternity passes as I wait, but he drags on his cigarette a few times more while looking in our direction.

I'm thinking "he." Natasha and Viktoria don't smoke. They never smell like smoke. I'd know since I'm allergic to smoke. This person is shorter than either one of them.

Who is this? Doesn't matter I must kill.

His sudden unsettling chuckle rattles me. I'm straining to stay still.

My heart no longer hammers inside my chest. It's now running the 100 yard dash at warp speed.

Sweat pools around the clutched-too-tight butcher knife, undermining my confidence.

The chuckle changes to ribald laughter and waves of it fill the room.

His hand covers his mouth to restrain the noise as he stares intently at the bed.

My own sweat and heart could kill me at this point!

He walks to the side of the bed. I feel and smell his presence next to me.

My eyelids twitch as I struggle to keep them closed. I test my grip on the knife.

Just lean over, and I'll give you a fatal surprise!

Moving ever so slightly to adjust my body, I hope to force a reaction on his part. And, it does.

My barely peeking eyes see him spin around and head for the door.

And I see it…revealed by a shard of light.

He has a ponytail!

Chapter 38

I lie perfectly still, still peeking, until I hear the front door lock.

What the fuck! Is it him? I didn't think things could get worse! He knows about Ethan's release. He knows Ethan's first stop—us.

I navigate slowly, with weapons in hand, to the light switch. Flipping it on, I glance around the kitchen and living room.

No Ponytail. Nothing disturbed.

I check my defensive stash, grabbing a roll of toilet paper and a towel along the way. Going into the kitchen, I start a pan of tea, tying the towel around a chair and placing the toilet paper roll in the middle of the table.

I sit at the table and massage my forehead with both hands. Tears form and vanish just as quickly—no time, no energy for that.

He's out for revenge obviously because we humiliated him in front of his gang.

Jail and prison not enough to pacify him! He can find out about Ethan by using the prison system, through a bribed guard, a prisoner/friend or an imprisoned family member.

But how did he find me and Zack?

Maybe, Viktoria is helping him…

My tears gain traction this time as I consider Zack's fate as a twice-orphaned child, if he isn't killed.

What stopped him from destroying our adoption in the first place? Above all, why didn't he strike this morning? Is he waiting for Ethan to arrive?

***

Zack sits in my lap as I feed him an early dinner. Since we played all afternoon, he's ready to eat. The Kefir nauseates me as I watch him slurp it down in bottle form. The television makes silent pictures in the living room. Ever on the alert now, I think about where I'd hide him. No place and no one come to mind—not Natasha, not Ivan and not Viktoria. There is no choice. I must do this alone. I can't count on Natasha to stop by today. But if she does, maybe, she can take him to a church until I deal with this.

As I carry him from the kitchen to the living room, burping him once then twice. I hear the shuffling of feet at the front door. In a split second, I kiss Zack and put him down in his pillow-fenced space in the bedroom, placing the binky in his mouth. A sigh of relief escapes my lips as I see a book sitting next to him for extra company. Racing across the room, I pause at the doorway and turn to blow him a kiss. Pointing to my eye, then my heart and then him, I tell him for the millionth time in our shared language that I love him.

After flying to the front door, I listen. I wait and hope to hear the rustle of Natasha' mink coat.

Nothing!

Then, the heavy thud of boots sends a fiery stripe of hate down my spine. Snatching my tools, I stuff them in my pockets, pull the entry table closer toward me and begin to push the couch across the wall to block the door. When the couch bumps the table, I catch my breath, not wanting to give away any advantage of surprise. The lamp wobbles and stands, the wads of toilet paper lying discarded next to it. My breath returns sharply as the hate spills into my brain like a levee breached. My heart ticks like an over wound clock, the sound too loud and too fast.

Positioning myself where the door will crack open, I put the alcohol between me and the couch, leaning on the bottle. My right hand grips the lighter and my left holds the hairspray accelerant.

This should become the blowtorch that at least slows him down.

"Ehhh?"

A deep throaty chuckle answers my question.

I hear the key click in the door as I uncap the bottle of alcohol. Holding the hairspray accelerant in one hand and the lighter in the other, I'm ready to do battle. The door cracks, heaving and pushing follow. I allow just enough leeway to get a good shot at him.

What!

My jaw drops as I see his smile and the barrel of his gun.

No! I fight here and now!

Looking down, he moves toward the couch to push it out of the way.

Without blinking, I drop the lighter and grab the barrel of his gun, pulling him forward. A bullet rips through my stomach and the can of hair spray fires directly into his eyes. He hunches over and yelps as I continue my assault, his body sideways to mine. Grabbing the about to-fall-bottle of alcohol, I splash him, a killer at a crime scene wielding a can of gasoline not more determined or deliberate. With my eyes trained on him, I grope for the lighter. My peripheral vision catches sight of it. And, once again, the toilet paper comes into view.

Another tool for me.

Snatching the lighter, my blowtorch becomes complete again. I set his clothes ablaze. Shrieking, he falls onto the couch, digging at his eyes and desperately trying to pat out the flames. The blood pours from my gut while Ponytail screams in agony, his body writhing and convulsing in pain.

A second voice joins his—Zack's. My weakening body, once like molten liquid, morphs now titanium strong with willpower. A cocktail of adrenalin and confidence empties into my veins. A quick thought back to my riding accident—the hideous accident, grisly recovery and return to the saddle, jumping horses and winning.

Walking backwards to the kitchen with my eyes fixed on him, I hook the towel-wrapped chair with my hand, pulling it toward the window. With a flick of the lighter, I torch the chair and throw it at the window. By leaning back and shifting my weight into the small wooden kitchen table, I manage to push it to the window and upend it out to the street below. Glass and embers scatter in its fiery wake, a beacon and a signal to anyone on the street. Cold wind and snow swishes into the room. Blood trickles through my fingers as I listen for Zack again.

A charred figure of a person approaches me with a needle in his hand. His face is black, bleeding, raw and melted like candle wax. Flakes of his burnt clothing scatter—an aura of char grilled evil as he walks toward me. His scent hangs in the air. I smell beef and pork frying in a pan seasoned with burning hair. Spinning around, I grab the pitcher from the counter and uncap it. Holding it in one hand, I stand fixated.

"*Da*, I have plans for you. You not die. Maybe, your baby die. Children sold here for body parts. Maybe, some rich baby needs new heart. Maybe, Viktoria make money finding new family for him. I don't care about baby. I make sure you live so you be a whore that works for me. "He laughs—his eyes dark holes tunneled into his head.

Glaring at me, he wipes his brow. A thick layer of skin falls from his hand. His skin now hangs by a chord from his brow. Unmoved, he continues toward me.

"Are you going to kill me with a metal pitcher?" he sneers.

I stand my ground, wielding my weapon.

Suddenly, he lunges at me with the needle, I move to the side, but it isn't enough. He grabs my left arm, plunging the needle into my bicep.

"My crack whore. Welcome to your new life."

Zack cries reach a shrill pitch now.

Without hesitation, I hit his hand with the pitcher. While bleach spills onto his raw bloody appendage, the needle sinks deeper into my arm. Screaming, he releases my arm. Instantly, I claw the empty needle away.

Clutching his hand and arm, roaring rage fills his eyes.

"Maybe, you won't get that far after all."

"You think!" With a half turn, I hurl the contents of the pitcher at his face. In a flash, I step back a few steps, watching the bleach arc across his hands, arms and face.

Skin once raw and charred is now bubbling as he yelps in anguish. Falling to the floor, he curls up in a fetal position, digging at his eyes.

My chance to get Zack and escape is now!

I inch my way to the bedroom, knowing I need a belt to slow blood loss, knowing double vision is distorting my clear path.

Opening the door, I see red-faced, teary-eyed Zack, his tiny fists clenched at his sides.

"Mommy's here," I tell him as I move to stroke his little head.

Not much gas left in the tank. Can only bend over once for you.

Hunting around for a belt, I see two on the dresser. Grabbing one, I place it over my clothes and above my waist—cinching it tightly—hoping it's enough to be an effective tourniquet.

Could be a flesh wound. Doesn't matter—have to save him. Breathing in and out, I test the fit, dizziness starting to set-in with each deep breath.

Grabbing a coat from a chair and a blanket from the bed, I wiggle slowly into it, leaving it open. Leaning over, I place the blanket on Zack. My knees buckle as I position the blanket under his neck. Reaching for the bedpost for support, I pause.

Glancing at my stomach, I see red from waist to hips, a mix of darker and lighter red.

I endured something this horrible before. I can absolutely do this!

Clenching the bedpost with one hand, I scoop Zack up with the other.

Heaving and gripping, I struggle to hoist him up to my shoulder.

Another pause as he leans into my shoulder, blubbering. I push-off from the bedpost and soldier toward the front door.

Sirens whine in the distance as I stare at my blocked exit.

Chapter 39

Immediately, my thoughts revert to Ponytail as we enter the living room. Seeing that he's still immobilized, I have to deal with the door, without zapping all my strength.

Approaching the entryway, I see the gun on the floor. I grit my teeth as I walk by it. I want that gun, but I can't chance bending over again. The couch partially blocks the door. If he squeezed through it, maybe, so can we.

With Zack in my arms, I cup his head and body as I squeeze us sideways into the opening. By leaning my back into the doorframe, I squat down, bringing up my knees against the door to pry it open just enough.

I sigh, pausing for another breath as we stand outside the apartment for the first time in a long time.

Now, have to go downstairs, such a possible, impossible task.

Clutching Zack tightly against my chest, I lean backward, feeling forward for the two hand rails that appear before me.

I can do this. It's about balance. I balanced over 5 foot fences, over multiple 3'6" fences on horseback. I'm an expert on balance. Take small slow steps while gripping the handrail. No looking down, just like jumping. Look straight ahead.

With a clenched jaw and a steady grip, we make it to the sidewalk. Nausea and an ever- increasing black darkness battle with me for control. Another pause as I turn the handle and push into the front door with my shoulder. Out on the street, I see people clustered to my right, pointing up and staring in shock. The chair and table are splintered—burning in a heap on the sidewalk—as icicles of glass dot the snowy perimeter. The sun disappears from the horizon as if seeking rest from a too long factory shift, relinquishing its job of illumination to the burning pile and the soon-to-be-here sirens. Following their gaze upward, I see disfigured Ponytail standing at the shattered kitchen window, his sunglasses scanning the crowd below. His half smile signals that he sees us.

Must try to run—run for the lives of my baby and me. Need to find a church. They can protect him if I can't.

One foot then the other sinks into the crunchy deep snow, the blood flowing faster now as I pump my arms and legs with every shred of strength.

From the corner of my eye, I notice a white van slows and shadows me street side. I push harder the blood, streaming like urine, wetting my clothes again. The van stops and people vault out, rushing toward me. My body shivers and trembles as I search for a church. The big black shadow growing, obstructing my vision, now only tunnel vision left. Cars are honking.

They aren't that loud. Maybe, it's because I'm breathing so hard.

Twinkling stars appearing now inside and outside the tunnel.

Someone stands in front of me, grabbing my arm.

Falling, backward. Backward, better for Zack.

I grip him harder to cushion his landing.

"Sophia, stay with me!"

Hallucinating—I hear Ethan. No, there is no Ethan. Drugs—only drugs do that. Focus.

"Please take my baby. Take care of him. I love him so," I beg.

Before my eyes close, I see a gun. And feel the pull of someone's hands on my shoulders.

213

Chapter 40

People are talking around me—I'm dead or dreaming.

"I'm so happy that she'll be ok!"

Ethan? Ethan squeezing my hand?

Zack. Zack okay?

"Our plans changed—huh, Natasha? We went from surprising her with the sight of gun-slinging me to her surprising us without a gun."

"*Spasibo*, Ivan for spotting her from the van. Please tell him, Natasha."

"Of course. She's tougher than I ever think. She make good Russian mother for him."

Yeah, I'm dead. She'd never say anything like that. Maybe, I'm in heaven now.

"I'm glad I shot Ponytail to death. I enjoyed it. Now, I have to try to stay out of prison."

"He shot and drug your wife. Much proof for us. No prison this time."

"What about her issue? When will she be herself again?"

Issue? What issue?

I can't shake myself awake! Maybe, post surgical hangover.

"Can she see the baby or be with him?"

"Doctor say no for now. He watch her for couple of days."

"Crack—very addictive. He say no treatment here."

No mention of Zack. He must be ok, getting re-acquainted with his Dad. What a relief!

"Did the doctor say what we should expect from her?"

"Violent anger, extreme insomnia and irritable."

Wonderful. At least, I'm alive, so much to be thankful for.

"Maybe, she needs that."

"Why? What do you say?"

"Viktoria is still loose, may be on the run, may be not. She's still a threat to us. By now, she knows the plan failed. Maybe, she was just an accomplice or maybe she was much more."

"Why—we can hire a guard. The police still look for her."

"That's probably not enough. Guards or police guards can be bribed."

"After all of this, she could still be in harm's way."

***

Days pass in the room—at first, hazy then not. There are sickeningly clear days when nausea and vomiting devour my day. Pains twist then torques every fiber of muscle, and convulsions follow that grip my body in malicious play. Anger flames when I turn to the dark side, thinking that I may still be a risk to my family and with my family, thinking that Methadone won't work for me, knowing that I can't even hold Zack unsupervised.

And I hate this crappy food! And someone feeding me this crappy food. And being tied to the bed rails. Guess they consider me dangerous since I damaged Mr. Mafia.

Taking stock of my surroundings, I see beige walls and beige tile covering the floors, and a large square window facing the street. To my left, the door to the room is closed. I look to the right along the long wall, another door to the bathroom. A vase containing yellow roses and a few speared, foil-wrapped hearts sits by the bed on a nightstand, a token of love from still Saudi-stationed Dad. A metal utilitarian drafting light flanks me on the other side attached to the headboard rail.

Lying in bed, my eyes focus on the window filled with spotlighting sunshine, and my ears listen to the hustle bustle of the staff as they prepare for the busy lunch hour. Two roaches breed on the wall next to the window frame as another skitters out of the bathroom.

And they wonder why I don't eat. If I enjoyed roach filth, maybe I would. I guess I should disregard the fact that those buggers can crawl on my sheets while I sleep. Of course, I shouldn't have an insomnia issue.

And depression. The big "D" word. I think some PTSD may be bubbling up in this pristine palace. Bottom line—if Zack is ok, I'm ok. I can choke down everything else. I really have a lot to be thankful for. I'd rather be in this roach-riddled hospital than dead in the snow.

A soft knock at the door disrupts the roach porn, sending them scattering in different directions.

"Hey, Sophia, I brought you something special for lunch." Ethan coos as he pushes open the door. Scrumptious sturgeon and Ethan's sexy smile brighten the room and lighten my morose mood. Sitting down the foil wrapped plate, he leans over to untie my tethers and hug me.

"This should be the last day you have to deal with these."

Rubbing my wrists, I smile at him and lean over to peck his lips.

"You're the best husband, Ethan!"

Sitting upright now, I flatten the covers and sheets to make way for the soon-to-be devoured meal.

"How's Zack? "I ask excitedly.

"He's fun and funny. He misses you, we both do," he says leaning toward me pushing my hair away from my face, his hand pausing before grazing my jaw line.

"When can I bail? Do you know?" My voice raises an octave as I think about the prospect.

"Doc said in a day or two," Ethan announces with a wink.

"Yesss! And I'm ready to go! I'm ready to pack tonight!"

"By the way, whose idea was it to bring the gun to me? Was it Natasha's?"

"No, your Dad called to make that request. He thought it'd be a good idea, and it was! He's on his way here," Ethan answers with a look of admiration.

"And what about Viktoria? Where is she? In jail?" I ask between bites of sturgeon.

Clearing his throat, he averts my gaze, and his eyes study the window.

"Uhh... We don't know where she is. When they find her, she'll face charges as an accessory," he says as sadness coats his every word.

"And both of you are safe?" I continue.

"Yes, and a policeman sits outside your door to keep you safe."

"Hmmmm...Since bribes are commonplace here, think I'll stay alert."

"Do you still have that gun?" I ask as I stab the sturgeon with my knife.

Chapter 41

With a hug and kiss, Ethan leaves me to return to Zack. Ivan is caring for him at Natasha's insistence. The sun skulks over the horizon and prisms of light and dark stream into the room. Evening is approaching. Sitting upright untethered in bed, I reach under my pillow to check for the gun, the black 9 mm has a full clip. Grabbing it, I carry it to the bathroom with me, the folds of my oversized hospital gown easily disguising its presence.

This is probably my last night here. I'm taking no risks, leaving nothing to chance.

As I walk out the door of the bathroom, I see a nurse setting down a tray, her back facing me. It's early for dinner, and my meds arrive with dinner.

My finger pushes the safety off as I walk slowly toward the bed. My hand grips the gun. My breathing slows as my chest pumps in distress.

A she turns around, I see Viktoria's face, framed by black hair.

I raise my gun leveling it at her. Her lack of surprise startles me.

"I knew you'd be armed. Shoot me now if you want."

"Move away from the tray. Empty your pockets and show me your hands."

My eyes search for signs of hidden weapons while hate pools in my throat.

Viktoria carefully complies her unblinking eyes meeting mine, her brows knitted in fear.

"Okay, move over to the chair. Sit there. I've got some questions for you."

"Why do you work with Ponytail?" My voice cracks as I try to control my fury.

"His name is Andrei. I desperately need money. He desperately need revenge," she answers as her eyes bore into mine.

"What exactly were you planning to do with our son?" I spit as I chamber a bullet, my gaze unflinching.

"The plan—you would be missing from the apartment when Natasha went to see you. He would force you to write a note saying you can't handle the situation anymore, saying that you abandon your baby. I write it for Ponytail, but he has to make sure it was the same note I wrote, letter by letter. "

"He would call me when you are not conscious. He planned to beat you, rape you, drug you and roll you in a rug. Then, he would carry you out on his shoulder and call me as he shut the door. Then, I go to apartment for baby. He does not want baby, only revenge with you." She reports.

"Again, what would you do with Zack?"

I want to kill her, but I have to know the whole story.

"I would ransom him to Natasha or find another family for him for money. Andrei help me do this without problems from Mafia."

My body trembles unable to contain the rattling rage that grips it. Monstrous anger claws at my insides in an attempt to escape and destroy.

"I am ashamed and sorry. I hate myself for my actions. I come to you without a weapon to say that. If you kill me, I am ready for that." Tears fill her eyes as she meets mine moment-for-moment.

"Why did they let us adopt Zack? They could have stopped us before it happened."

"I ask Andrei that too. Mikhail ordered him to leave the baby alone. Mikhail grew up in a child house. He wants to see your baby have a better life. He controls child houses, but he never sees those children. They become numbers to him on a piece of paper. He saw pictures of your baby. He thinks Andrei would be satisfied since Ethan is in prison. He thinks that would be enough for him."

"Now, tell me why I shouldn't kill you?" I hiss.

Tears stream down her red face as it twists in grief.

"I don't have a good answer for you," she whines.

"I didn't think so. Turn around and walk to the window. And stop at the window." Urine pools at her feet as she shifts her weight back and forth.

At my bed now—eyes focused on her, I press the button for assistance as she cranes her neck around for a peek.

"Yes, I'd like nothing better than to shoot you as you stand for all the heartache we suffered. I could kill you, making it look like self-defense, but I won't. I'm not Mafioso, and I won't act like them. You'll be punished with prison or jail time, that's enough justice for us."

Viktoria's grim tear-streaked face, tells me without words, that she'd rather die now.

A nurse opening the door interrupts our silent speeches to one another. Surprise registers on her too long face and shock in her too white eyes as she processes the scene.

"Turn around and tell her. Tell her that you are the one the police are looking for," I instruct while lowering my gun.

Finally, I can look forward to going home.

Chapter 42

The sun warms my skin, waking me to the dawn of the first day back with my family. Ethan is at my bedside with Zack, both are smiling, lighting up the room. Shouldering Zack, Ethan pecks me on the lips and then places Zack on my chest. His little hands feel my face. He voices his approval with a raspberry and a hug.

"Everything getting back to normal, huh?" Ethan observes.

While Zack yanks my hair and bounces on my chest, Ethan packs for me.

A soft knock before the door inches open. Natasha stands in the entryway holding my breakfast tray.

"I ask the nurse if I can bring this to you," she says with a half smile.

"The drugs, they gave me, must have hallucinogenic side effects. I see Natasha carrying my breakfast tray."

"You feeling better. You trying to be funny," she quips sourly.

"Anyway, we talk while you eat," she says as she sets the tray down in front of me.

"Apartment window is repaired. You go to apartment today because you must go to American Embassy tomorrow to obtain Visa for Zack. It's the final step before you leave."

***

Everyone is asleep, but me. The sun peeks through the curtains to announce the start of the day. I glance at Zack and fluff my barrier pillow before rolling out of bed. Leaning over Ethan as he sleeps, I kiss his lips lightly.

"Hey, Ethan, time to wake-up. Today, we go to the US Embassy."

Balling his fists and stretching, he smiles.

"The last stop in Russia before we go home. What a great feeling!"

"With the "book" of documents we have, it should be no more difficult than changing a diaper," he comments as he laces his hands together behind his head.

"Ivan will be here at 7:30 to drive us there and help us. Natasha says he'll drive us there and wait," I say as I reach for Zack.

***

The intended destination soon becomes clear—a tall, beige building which manages to standout, only due to the unusual uniforms of the military guards flanking the entry way. A large group of people waits impatiently outside the front door. Ivan uses the van to part the crowd as he proceeds to parallel park as close as possible to the front entrance of the building. As we walk to the entrance on slippery cement and earth, the mob offers no courtesy, no civility. Like concertgoers clamoring to move inside the gate, the throng pushes and compresses. With a growl, Ivan begins shoving his way through the mass like an enraged bear. As we enter the checkpoint area, one of several soldiers motions us his way.

"Passports please," the soldier asks curtly.

"We're here for our Visa appointment at 8 am," I say, handing him my passport. After glancing at my passport and me, he uses a green light to check for a watermark; then, waves Zack and me ahead. I walk a few steps and wait for the others.

"And yours, sir," he says as he studies Ethan.

"Of course, sir," Ethan says, only too happy to comply.

"By the way, this is our friend, Ivan, who travels with us in Russia. He's a Russian citizen, and he's here to help us."

After the scrutiny ends, he waves Ethan ahead, and Ivan steps up to take his place.

"*Nyet*! You cannot enter. You must leave," the soldier says as he drops his right shoulder allowing his AK-47 to fall across his chest. He points to the door, waiting for Ivan to disappear.

"What a surprise! Didn't expect that, but it makes sense," I mutter.

"Me, neither. He'll have to go back to the van and wait. I hope it won't take too long."

"Do you realize that we're on our own again? The last time was in the bar. I realize we're in the American Embassy, but I still feel uneasy. Natasha should be here with us."

"Remember, Sophia, we're in the American Embassy. I can't think of a safer, friendlier place for us. By the way, do you think Natasha would really help us with this? She's done more than enough already. Give her a break! We can handle this. She probably thinks we can handle this too."

Putting his arm around my waist, Ethan guides me to the nearest sentry who tells us where to go, his southern drawl more beautiful than coveted, diamond, chandelier earrings.

Walking through one narrow hallway to a series of large waiting rooms, we enter a vast room with wooden pews and a room filled with sad faces.

As I look from face to face, I see fire-forged intensity. A busy bus stop terminal filled with patrons, waiting for the tardy

Thanksgiving bus, couldn't be more dismal. Fatigue and desperation stamp every face. Several vignettes play out around us—a bleary-eyed couple book-ending four children, 2 brothers and 2 sisters; a man with a tortured expression cradling and rocking a young man in his lap, curled in a fetal position; a man who looks through me, and a man who doesn't meet my gaze.

Leaning toward Ethan, I whisper, "This doesn't look good, it looks terrible. Everyone is tattooed with anguish."

"After all we've been through, we can walk into that room and walk out with a Visa," Ethan mutters back, his voice cracking with concern.

His arm wraps around my waist as he gently pushes me into the next room. It's a smaller square room with perimeter seating and an entire wall with four bank teller-type windows. The lilting sing-song of Americans speaking English helps quell my uneasiness.

Easy Visa, fast flight home, easy Visa, fast flight home...

This room bubbles over with joyful chaos—crying babies, smiling babies, toddlers waddling from wall to wall shadowed by Mom or Dad. A jungle of activity all confined to one small area. Zack and I sit in one of the perimeter chairs while Ethan plows toward the skirmish at the teller windows. The din of casual chatter engulfs the room.

***

After nearly an hour of watching Ethan in line, I'm bored enough for small talk.

"So, who is that person with you? Everyone seems to have an extra person with them," I ask another American sitting in a chair nearby.

224

"Oh, that's our Russian mediator," says the woman. "He facilitates the Visa process by using his inside experience and knowledge."

"Don't you have one? You really should have one. I don't think you can get a Visa without one."

Damn!! We don't have one, and we don't have the money with us to hire one. No one told us that we needed one. Natasha probably doesn't know they exist.

Dismayed, I walk back to Ethan, he stands next in line.

"We've got a problem. Those extra people are mediators who facilitate the Visa process by using inside experience and knowledge. It seems to be the *modus operandi* here. This may be much more complicated than we expected. And since we didn't bring extra money, I don't think we have a chance of subcontracting one here."

"Let's see what they say. I'm here already at the front of the line," he says confidently.

We're this far along, and it's still wait and wonder.

"It'd be easier if you'd sit and watch from the sidelines," he says with a smile.

"If I stay by your side, she'll see our beautiful baby which may somehow make things easier for us. You can't wrestle the paperwork and the baby. Please," I beg.

"Okay, but keep your cool. This is not the time or place to be aggressive. Bureaucracy rules the day."

"Next," the teller announces as she stamps a document.

"My name is Ethan Evans. I'm here to obtain a Visa for my adopted Russian-born son."

The official at the teller window listens with a masklike expression. She glances around him, her eyes darting from left to right. Dissatisfied, she looks at him with a steely stare, her eyes now squinting.

"Where's your mediator?" she asks suspiciously, as she sits taller in her chair.

"We don't have a mediator. We didn't know we needed one. We didn't know mediators existed until a few minutes ago," Ethan responds sincerely.

The teller sits stupefied. No words needed because her face speaks for her, her mouth gaping in astonishment.

Staring blankly at him for a few minutes, she finally speaks.

"I don't even know what to say. I feel sorry for you."

"Maybe, we can make this work without a mediator...," she offers meekly.

"You need three copies of each document; then, I'll review the complete package again."

Ethan and I thank her profusely as we step out of the line.

"I think we'll be okay if we get three copies of each document. I should be able to get copies here in the Embassy. You stay here with Zack and wait. I'll take care of this in no time," he says before I can disagree. In a flash of color, he disappears.

This should be simple and quick. After all, we are Americans in the US Embassy.

Zack sleeps while I pass the time visiting with other parents. Occasionally, I glance at the wall clock. Minutes tick by.

This is taking a long time. It's been almost two hours. What's the problem?

Again, in a flash, Ethan reappears.

"Well, I know you didn't forget about us," I say lightheartedly.

But Ethan doesn't return my smile, he looks dismayed. "All of the people that I asked refused to let me use the copy machines. I have *zero* copies. I asked people on every floor of this building. I can't believe it!" Looking down at the floor, he shakes his head in exasperation.

"That's bewildering! Maybe, there's a different way?"

He won't look at me, only the floor as if it's a chalkboard of ideas.

"I've got it! You wait here while Ivan and I search for a commercial copy center."

"No," I say firmly. "We've been separated enough in Moscow as a family. I'm not sitting here, wondering and waiting. I've had too much experience with that. As much as I'd like to do it for you, the answer is no."

As Zack and I settle into the van, Ethan hops into the front seat, puts his hand to his ear to replicate a phone and utters Natasha's name. Ivan dials Natasha and hands the phone over.

"Natasha, please tell Ivan we need to find a commercial copy center," he says. "And we need to find it fast."

***

Ivan locates a copy center a few blocks from the Embassy. As we walk in the store, he takes charge, putting some of documents on the counter and asking for a price. Zack and I sit on the sidelines observing and waiting to return to the Embassy. When Ethan takes the documents and walks to a machine to begin, the store manager rushes toward him.

"*Nyet*, I make copy—only me," the manager declares.

With a roll of his eyes, Ethan hands him the documents and says, "They must stay in the same order, stapled in order for the Embassy."

Turning to Ivan, he makes the hand signal for the phone and says Natasha's name.

"Natasha, the store manager must make the copies. Will you tell him how important it is that the documents be in the same order and stapled the same way?"

"Yes, of course."

I smile as I think of what she might say to the store manager. He'll probably feel like a harpooned whale by the time she ends the conversation.

A few minutes after Ethan hands the phone to the store manager, I see him scowl as he holds the phone a few inches from his ear.

I never realized how much we have in common. I'd have done the same thing. She's a fighter like me. I bet she has to soften her rhetoric with extra cash.

In a huff, the store manager ends the conversation and gives the phone back to Ivan. With documents in hand, he storms to a back room to make the copies. Minutes pass. Finally, the manager returns with the documents and copies. He hands them over to Ivan who pays him.

As we walk out to the van, Ethan studies the documents.

"Shit! He jumbled the order. They're not stapled either," he yells.

This time, we all settle in the back seat of the van surrounded by snow banks of documents that we try to organize.

"The originals and translated documents are mismatched! I haven't even looked at the copies yet!" he shouts in frustration.

"It'd be safer to go back to the US Embassy and sort this out there in the parking lot rather than slog through this problem in the copy center parking lot," I suggest.

With a sigh, Ethan grabs the documents stack and jumps in the front seat, slamming the door behind him.

While Ivan looks to him for direction, Ethan uses his hands to turn an imaginary steering wheel.

"Ivan, *pagilista*, we have to go back to the Embassy," he says staring ahead.

***

In the Embassy parking lot, Ivan and Ethan settle into the backbench seat. Ivan locks the doors, and the heater warms the space. I sit behind the driver's seat feeding Zack a bottle as Ethan and Ivan try to separate and match documents.

"There are 40 originals plus three sets of copies. And I don't know how, with the language barrier, we'll do this. It has to be correct," Ethan fumes, running his hands through his hair.

"Wait I do know!" he exclaims. He continues. "We'll call Natasha. I'll read an English document to her and give the phone to Ivan who'll find the corresponding Russian document. We'll sort through this project page-by-page, but I think it'll work."

Hours tick by as the men crane over the mounds of documents. Finally, the perfectly collated Embassy package emerges.

At the Embassy, while standing at the teller window, Ethan shifts his weight nervously as the official audits the document package. I'm biting my lower lip as she slowly checks page after page.

"Well, you have the required three copies and then some. I've never seen some of these documents before. You actually have extra documents, unnecessary documents." Dusting her hands, she sets aside the package.

"Okay, this is good enough. I approve your Visa. You can pick it up later tonight."

Like a battered ship lost at sea, we finally arrive at the sun-drenched port.

Chapter 43

Today, we trek to the airport in a different car as per Natasha's instructions. Natasha declines our invitation to say good-bye at the airport, but she busies herself with the task of helping us prepare to go home. While Ethan and I pack, Natasha bundles-up Zack for the cold outdoors.

Ethan and I cluster around the large open Tumi suitcase, scratching our heads, dumbfounded as to how to pack everything.

"Let's see Russian chocolate, honey, vodka, books and *Matryoshka* dolls. Check!"

With a loud sigh, Natasha puts Zack in Ethan's arms and re-positions the gifts in our suitcase.

"I travel much. This way should keep all safe."

Taking Zack back into her arms, she gives him a kiss followed by a bear hug before she turns her face away and wipes her eyes.

"*Spasibo*, Natasha from all of us."

"You are ready to go now," she says dabbing at her still flowing tears.

"I have one last question. Why can't we use the van?" I ask wanting to know but not.

"Sugar in gas tank. It obvious someone angry with you. You on list for revenge."

A sinkhole of sadness opens up in the room, taking our glow, our smiles and our optimism with it.

"Are we safe?" Ethan asks hoarsely.

"As safe as we can make you." Closing her eyes for a moment, she places her finger on her forehead, concentrating.

"Stay together. Look at faces-anyone you seen at bar."

Peering out of the kitchen window, she continues.

"Keep luggage at your side always."

"Now, it time to go."

Walking to the door of the apartment, she holds it open for us.

"Ivan stay with car downstairs and waits for you."

Following us downstairs to street side, she takes Zack from Ethan's arms and takes him to Ivan to hold while we settle into the van.

Now, seated—baby in my arms, I turn to thank her again, but she's gone.

Craning my neck around, I see her running through the snow—away from us.

***

At the airport, I hug Ivan and Ethan shakes his hand as we say our good-byes before boarding the plane bound for London. Ever alert, we stay close together, like nervous cats hunted by coyotes. At the gate, we stand next to the check-in counter, a small comfort should a brawl occur.

Finally, we walk through the gate to the Tarmac to board the plane. Just as we settle into our seats, Zack begins to cry, toys and bottles don't appease him. In desperation, Ethan walks up and down the aisle with him as he wails, now the faces around us morphing from irritable frowns to stares and scowls.

As Ethan passes by a black man with dreadlocks cuddling his own baby, he pauses. The two men begin talking and Ethan motions me over. After visiting with us for a few minutes, he sings to Zack, calming him immediately. In a matter of minutes, Zack relaxes enough to sleep.

I hear applause around us as the other passengers respond, grateful for the fact some solitude may exist on this journey.

"You should take a bow! That was amazing! You sing so beautifully! Your voice is better than Benadryl. Thank you so very much!" I gush.

"Thanks. We're lucky to be flying with you, a smart parent and a good singer. Do you sing professionally?" Ethan questions.

"Yes, I do in Russia. I'm popular as a singer and as the spouse of the US Ambassador to New Zealand, an unusual combination," he answers with a broad smile, displaying his perfect dazzling teeth.

Several hours later, Zack awakens. I kiss his soft head and place him sideways in my lap. I kiss his tiny hands and uncurl his fingers, as fragile and soft as tendrils, and kiss each one just below the tiny slivers of fingernails. Grabbing my index finger, he squeezes and smiles. I reposition him, kissing his little hands away, and lay him against my shoulder for a big hug. He begins to cry and I offer him a bottle, which he quickly pushes away as the odor of a foul diaper fogs our space.

"Wow, what did you eat? Pureed liver and onions? Your dirty diaper could send people screaming for the exits with mouths covered," Ethan jokes.

"Well, why don't you change his diaper, funny guy?" I ask.

"Okay, no problem. I'll *teach you* how to minimize the stench and the mess. See you in a few."

Reaching over and scooping Zack into his arms, he walks to the bathroom.

That cramped airplane bathroom, the metal cylinder bathroom, with only enough room to turn around, flush and walk a measured step to the mirrored sink. It makes me feel like I stepped into a can of hairspray with metal walls and a metal toilet to relieve myself. If there was no cabin noise, it could be too revealing...

I stare out the window of the plane, thinking about our next stop and the day ahead of us. A loud scream of horror reverberates throughout the plane. Jerking up from my chair as if pulled by a puppeteer, I bolt down the aisle as the tormented shrieking continues.

What's going on? That's Zack's scream coming from the bathroom!

Just a few steps more...Ethan opens the door, looking surprised to see me.

"That was terrible! Why is he screaming?"

"He's never cries like that. Something went horribly wrong in there."

"What happened?" I question, my teeth grind ready to shred.

Ethan looks hurt that I would say that. I know he's careful with our baby, but Zack cried as if he was being slapped.

Red-faced Ethan refuses to meet my eyes, instead choosing to look straight ahead.

"I laid him on the metal counter to change his diaper. It frightened him and the small metal space amplified his crying," he answers in a whispery tone.

Zack nuzzles into Ethan's shoulder as he walks indignantly toward our seats. Following a few steps behind, I become suddenly aware of the spectacle we created in the cabin filled with onlookers.

A 30ish dishwater blonde mom and her teenage daughter whisper back and forth, covering their mouths as if discussing a secret code. The 50ish red head with a sheaf of paperwork in her hand glares at us with white-hot intensity, a twisted rope smile pasted on her lips. The silver-haired grandmother—who had just smiled at us with admiration when we boarded the plane—sits now with western novel interrupted resting on her chest, gritting her teeth and focusing an accusatory brow at us. The weary executive stares at us, a mix of worry and disappointment contorting his face, nodding his head back and forth in reproach.

I've seen enough. I'm not meeting anyone's gaze. I'll just look straight ahead.

With all of the adoption horror stories in the international press lately… People notice. This is the Russian adoption route.

Embarrassed Ethan finally returns to his seat with Zack. The shrill silence fills the space between us until I lean into his shoulder. Zack sleeps contentedly on his other shoulder, the sun illuminating his angelic face.

The flight attendant appears almost instantly, waving a white paper napkin like a surrender flag.

Bad news or good news?

"Any drink requests from this group?"

I would drink liquor from a 100-gallon livestock tank now.

"Vodka and cranberry juice for both of us," Ethan requests, a sigh of relief punctuating his order.

Since Zack began to walk in the apartment, he bawls, upset about his loss of liberty. Toys and walking jaunts, back and forth along the aisles, and the bottles don't appease him. And unfortunately, the Singer said his goodbyes at the last stop.

Again and again, the sympathetic flight attendant approaches us with mixed drinks which we uncharacteristically guzzle like glasses of water. Finally, after enduring another ear-piercing episode, the attendant decides to serve us again immediately.

This time, he adds, "I think you really need these".

Chapter 44

The flight from London to the US passes—pleasantly, uneventfully. Zack rarely cries and spends his waking hours testing the destructibility of his toys. Ethan and I marvel at his play like two devoted sports fans ogling at a play-off game.

After disembarking, our first stop is customs. The colorful clean airport terminal winks at us as if gold dusts our surroundings. Overjoyed to touch rich US soil, we actually enjoy our interaction with customs agents. The drug dog sniffs our luggage, making an extra pass by the gift bag. Passing through our second checkpoint, we walk with baby and luggage through a roped area to an awaiting metal door. With a quick, easy push, the door opens to a group of bedazzled family and friends.

Zack seems dazed as my father pulls him close for a hug. He reluctantly accepts the affection engulfing him, but quickly expresses interest in returning to my arms to assess the situation. Locking his legs around my upper body, he signals that we should happily proceed as one body, mine carrying his. The weight of the moment weakens my knees and sends tingles up my spine. My heart beats wildly as the reality sets in. The emotional and financial marathon that led us through 12 time zones ends now. The finality of the moment quashes my composure, and tears of relief and exhilaration flood my face.

We finally crossed the finish line! I could kiss the terminal floor! This is one of the most euphoric moments of my life!

***

Zack sits in a car seat, its firm hug completely infuriating him. He cries relentlessly, the sense of confinement and confusion at not being held is too much. A half hour into our trip, Zack sleeps comfortably in his car seat, the ensuing quiet allowing us to reflect upon and embrace this extraordinary event. And I can't help but think.

After this trip, nothing can rattle us!

As the sun showers the day with sunlight for the last time, we begin unpacking our suitcases. Zack sleeps his mouth agape, a string of drool attaching him to his pillow.

We scurry from one room to the next, putting clothes in the hamper, shoes in the closet and documents in the study.

I rub my hands like a greedy miser as I prepare to open the "gift" suitcase, untouched since we left the apartment.

Mmmmmm…Russian chocolate and honey…..I can taste them now.

A quick *zzzzzzzzzzzzzzzzzzzzzzzzzzzip…*and a sweet smile shifts sour.

"What the hell!" I howl.

"Ethan, will you look at this!"

I rub my eyes and peer into the suitcase again.

The vodka bottles are broken—soaking everything within reach, the jars of honey smashed—shellacking splinters of glass like butterflies in a frame. And my bullion bars of chocolate are unwrapped.

"What the fuck!" I screech.

As I pick up a precious bar with pincer-like fingers, I see that someone has bitten into it. All of them unwrapped, all contaminated by a single bite.

If this person just wanted to destroy my chocolate, they could just let the splintered glass and vodka do the dirty work, but I bet they bit the chocolate first then smashed the rest.

"WHY WOULD SOMEONE WANT TO DO THIS?" I roar.

Ethan rushes to my side, his slack-jawed look speaking for him.

Carefully, we pick through the gooey drippy chocolate.

"I packed gift books in there and extra powdered formula for Zack," I assess as my hands search the messy mass of destroyed gifts. Picking up one children's book of nursery rhymes pickled in vodka, I shake it, reluctantly opening it to check the pages.

Ethan stands statue-still, his "hard" eyes heating up with hate.

"THEY'RE ALL RUINED! Zack's new Russian storybooks bleed ink, vodka and honey. Why?" I mutter, confused.

While my mind cycles into analytical aerials of what ifs, my hands, hands that look like mine but don't feel connected to my body, methodically keep searching for … the powdered formula.

And there it is… in its airtight container, the lip of the lid curled up on one side.

I'm sure it's contaminated. I'll just toss it.

As my hand clutches it, the honey-coated container clings to my hand.

Looking at the side of the transparent container, I notice a too dark substance. A mixture of white powder formula, honey and vodka shouldn't be dark.

It looks green—dark green! And it smells pungent powerful and herbal.

As I pop the lid, I see a bag of leafy greens and a few rolled cigarettes.

"It's Pot! Someone put pot in our bag and…" My non-finger fingers keep sifting through the contents in the container.

"And mini bags of white crystal powder. I… bet that's cocaine!"

"Someone tried to bust us, not use us as "Mules" as if that were any better. The quantity of drugs is so small," Ethan observes as he strokes his chin.

"How did our suitcase manage to slip through?" I wonder aloud.

"Well, the contents of most suitcases aren't soaked in vodka. Maybe that camouflaged the scent of the drugs to the dogs. Or… it could be a miss," he says as he massages his forehead with his fingers.

"It happens more often than you'd think. I read a story a while back about drug K-9s. Only one out of ten K-9 teams are efficient enough to detect contraband due to improper training."

"Lucky? We were … lucky, and got the B team? Lady Luck stands in our corner now. What a relief, but I think the stash was a parting shot from the Mafia. In fact, I…"

Sitting on the bed now, holding the container, I take a moment to scratch my forehead.

"I think they sabotaged the van with sugar as payback for Ponytail. And I think they have "connections/eyes" at the airport. Obviously, they've been watching us."

"I a..gree," Ethan stammers, his face showing horror.

"Don't say it!" He blurts out.

"Do you realize the stash could've put us in prison and Zack…?"

The possibilities of what could have been storm through my mind.

***

The established neighborhood is country quiet in direct juxtaposition to its location, a busy important sector of the city bordering a medical center. It surprises me to have peace and quiet so close to the heart of the city. Two story New Orleans style homes, built 80 years ago, line the streets on both sides. A large oak graces every front yard, creating a shaded arbor of kissing trees over the street. At the end of the street, cars whizz by on Mopac Expressway-a major artery in the city. Mimi's house now our house, just the way she wanted it. Mimi's wish to meet her grandchild met, a few days before she died

***

Today, we're going to a different part of the city—to the stables. The emerald green pastures visible from the freeway. A stretch of white 4-plank fence bookends the mile long entry road on either side. As I turn on to the road, I slow the car to a crawl and lower the windows. Hundred-year old oaks rustle in the breeze like several southern belles sashaying in bulbous, rainbow-colored taffeta skirts. Lounging areas dot the landscape like sitting areas surrounding a grand checkered ballroom floor. Tradition, as absolute as the thirteen colonies, and affluence dance a time-tested waltz all the while winking with impunity at the impossible-to-fault aesthetics. The clean air, the freshly mowed green grass and the smell of pine beckon us into the all white barn, not a barn but a balm for anything that hurts. Zack hangs over my shoulder—his eyes glazed with wonder as we walk to my horse's stall.

My bay mare, Isabella, pokes her head out of the stall window to greet us. I caress her nose softly with my hand while cooing her name. Nickering back at me, she watches with eyes half-closed as I take Zack's little hand, covering it with mine, to touch her nose.

Stretching my fingers and then cupping them tightly, I stroke her head gently. And she lowers her head respectfully.

Zack giggles as he touches her velvety muzzle, his face glowing with warmth.

"Yeah, baby, that's what she does for me too."

***

Isabella completes the hunter course with effortless fluidity—a Mallard landing on a lake not as artful. She joyfully jumps over each obstacle as if it holds more promise of pleasure than green grass. As we walk around the arena to cool off, I think gratefully about second chances, second challenges and second victories. I realize that my life isn't bound in a burlap bag of fear and what ifs; instead, it's swathed in an evening gown of silky comfort and glittery triumph.

Life without Zack would be second-rate, a life thinly lived instead of a life richly chosen and abundantly experienced. And I would endure the adoption freefall all over again to be Zack's Mom.

Author Interview Questions

Have you traveled to Russia?
Yes, I have.

What did you most enjoy about writing this novel?
Spotlighting the strength of the human spirit, showing that there's a way to thwart danger, while locked in an apartment, without the luxury of a cell phone, home phone or gun.

What did you least like about writing this book?
I hated to write the bar scene because it had to be dark, violent and gritty.

Do you want to add any other comments about the bar scene?
I based the violence on true stories, not some dark twisted corner of my mind, which makes the scene more terrifying. I spent hours in front of a computer to do research for this book.

With so many books on the market, why should readers buy *Beautiful Evil Winter*?
Read *Beautiful Evil Winter* because it offers the opportunity to travel to one of the most dangerous countries in the world, to live the frightening experience of being unwittingly caught in the crosshairs of the Mafia, to add Suspense, a dash of Thriller and Romance Sizzle to a day and finally, to enjoy a Multi-Award-Winning novel.

Why did you decide to write this book?

The idea resonated with me over and over again. Not only did it top my bucket list, but it nagged me daily. I kept a diary after returning from Russia with our adopted son. Since I thought the experience would make a great story, I wrote a memoir. When I learned that, unless an author can claim celebrity status, a memoir has little if no chance of being well read, I changed my outlook on my mostly yawner of a story and molded it as an Action Thriller.

I believe writing a book that suits the author's tastes helps pave the road to success. Commitment to the writing craft, commitment to the marketing, commitment to telling a standout story become easier when the author feels that the story must be told. I believe an undying passion for the story tethers the author to strive for a standard of excellence. And as Toni Morrison said, "If there's a book that you want to read, but it hasn't been written yet, then you must write it."

What takeaway message does this book offer?

When someone can speak of tragedy, in some way, as a triumph of the human spirit, a sense of empowerment flourishes fortifies and life's trajectory forever changes.

What is important for aspiring authors to know as they begin their journey?

Be prepared for a marathon not a sprint if you want to be an established author. Read books about writing, like Stephen King's *On Writing*, enroll in a quality on-line class, I recommend UCLA Extension Writers' Program. Respect the craft by studying it, as if mandated, to have the tools to tell a story in the most optimal way. As Stephen King said, "If you don't have the time to read, you don't have the time (or the tools) to write. Simple as that."

Have you completed your second novel?
Yes, I expect it to be available in January of 2015. My second novel is another Action Thriller hybrid; however, it will be based in the US.

What do you enjoy doing in your spare time?
Read, ride my horse and take my Pyrenees, a Therapet dog-in-training, to class.

Visit www.kellyklavenderauthor.com for more information about Kelly's novels.

To enter the quarterly giveaway to win an autographed paperback copy of one of Kelly's novels, send an e-mail to kellyklavender@gmail.com and request that your name be added to list.

Thank you for joining me on this journey!

Truly,

Keely K. Lavender

CPSIA information can be obtained at www.ICGtesting.com
Printed in the USA
LVOW10s2033101114

412966LV00003B/6/P